Man of Her Dreams

By Cathie Shaffer

DEDICATION

To Mark and Chloe. Here's to new adventures!

Prologue

The night was still, the courtyard lit only by a sliver of silver from the waning moon. The woman rose from the bed unable to sleep. The restlessness in her soul was heightened by the loneliness of the stone walls below her and the pervasive quiet, a change from the usual wind that blew across the flat land surrounding the castle.

She wandered through the room, waging a battle against a sudden longing to stroll out into the dark. What was wrong with her tonight, she wondered. The tall carved bed, the fire smoldering on the hearth across the room, the relief of being free of prying eyes at last - these things usually calmed her and prepared her for the day ahead. Tonight they reminded her only that while others loved and argued, teased and lusted, she wore the yoke of responsibility. She knew the consequences to foolish behavior, even at the tender age of sixteen. She was her father's only child, and the duty of keeping this manse efficiently operating during his increasingly frequent absences fell to her.

Mayhap it had been the wine at dinner. Mayhap it had been tainted. Or it might have been the secretive smile on the face of Anne, her maid, as she'd dressed her in her nightclothes that evening. She'd seen that certain smile before. It no doubt meant Anne was planning to make good on the promises her flirtation had offered all day to a certain blue-eyed stable hand.

Or it had been him. The image of a strong, stalwart man flashed into her memory, his dark teasing eyes and a handsome face marred only slightly by the scarred reminder of a long-ago sword fight. He had come to deliver a message, nothing more. But she had known by his fine steed and his bearing that he was no mere messenger.

He was more, but what?

He hid secrets, but whose?

She sensed that with his arrival, her life had changed forever, but for good or bad, she did not know.

The blaring of the alarm clock brought Jessi Flint out of the dream and back into the humidity of the

August day. Bleary-eyed, she reached up and slammed it off. She'd gotten in from the airport too early this morning for the day to start like this.

Sighing, she rolled out of bed and started for the shower. But her mind wasn't on the full day ahead of her, but rather the dark eyes and upturned lips of the man in her dream. The man who'd populated her dreams since she was just a teenager.

The man she knew couldn't exist but pined for nevertheless.

Man of Her Dreams

Chapter One

"Destinee, get in here!"

There were a whole lot of things Jessi wasn't in the mood for. One was early calls, since she'd gotten home from Atlanta on a red eye at one this morning. Nor was she tempted to make cold calls on potential clients, since the ninety-degree heat had wilted her auburn curls into a mass of frizz.

Most of all, she was not in the mood for another of those little talks with her secretary. She liked to pride herself on being a kind and understanding boss, but this time Destinee had crossed the line.

More like jumped over it and erased it behind her.

"You need me, boss lady?" Destinee stepped in, her hoop earrings swaying as she tipped her head and waited for an answer.

"Give me one good reason not to fire you right now." Jessi grabbed an elegant gray notecard from the top of her desk, yanking it so hard the paper tore. Her green eyes flashed and narrowed as she tossed it across

Page 7

the desk to her one and only assistant.

Those same eyes darkened as Destinee said, "You asked me to go through the mail and take care of what needed to be done while you were gone."

"I meant set up appointments, send replacement certificates, things like that," Jessi hissed, trying hard to keep from shouting. She knew better than to do that around Destinee. "Think back. Didn't I give you very explicit instructions before I left? Like take care of the business mail and stack up my personal mail for me?"

"I heard what your outer persona said." Destinee wagged a finger at Jessi. "But I responded to your inner being, the child you continually repressed. How can you slam the door on your future when your inner being and your outer shell can't even agree on what's best for you?"

Jessi rolled her eyes. She'd known Destinee - just plain Debbie then - was a little eccentric when she hired her five years ago. Her offbeat behavior had been sort of charming at the time before she'd really gotten into this New Age mumbo-jumbo, all those crystals, herbs and what not.

She liked her, sure. You couldn't help but like

Destinee. The sole reason she still had a job was because she was a powerhouse secretary. She typed at warp speed, never lost a file and could charm even the most irate client into being put on hold. Moreover, she always managed to find a solution no matter how desperate a problem might seem, even if those solutions did go outside ordinary office practices sometimes.

Jessi had no time for a Destinee moment now. Instead she had to figure why for the first time ever, her secretary had deliberately done the opposite of what Jessi had asked. Over the years, they'd had differences of opinion, but Destinee had never ignored an order before. Whatever the problem, Jessi intended to get to the bottom of it.

"Before I left for New York, didn't I tell you I had no intention of going back to Durkin for my high school reunion?"

Destinee nodded, her perkiness ebbing under Jessi's glare.

"Didn't I tell you if I got an invitation, I'd take care of when I got back?"

Destinee nodded again, her shoulders slumping.

Still in control, but barely, Jessi asked "Then

why did I get a letter from our old class president telling me he's looking forward to seeing me again? And to meeting my fiancé when we get to Michigan?"

Destinee's lower lip began to quiver. "You're disturbing my aura, Jessi! I can't talk to you anymore until we both take some need deep cleansing breaths."

Tamping down an impatient sigh, Jessi began to breathe deeply in and out. She'd learned sometimes, if a serious conversation with Destinee was to go anywhere, you simply had to share the ritual of the day and get it over with. She breathed in and out, counting three on the in breath and five on the out breath, just as Destinee had taught her. To her surprise, she began to feel calmer. Which was a good thing. It was hard to carry on a civilized conversation with clenched teeth.

"I tried to do what you wanted, but I couldn't counteract fate." Destinee sneaked a quick peek at Jessi before dropping her eyes to the desk top again. "That letter came, and then your mother called, and that's when I knew what was supposed to happen."

Jessi dropped into her high-back leather office chair. No wonder things had gone haywire so fast. Destinee and her mother. Now there was a combination.

Alone, either one could drive her to distraction. Together, they made a padded room and a strait jacket seem appealing.

"What did you two talk about?" Jessi's tone was gentler.

"Your cousin Becky's wedding."

Jessi screeched with delight.

"Becky and Tim are getting married? I can't believe it. It's about time; they're not getting any younger. I can't imagine what took them so long."

"Oh, Jessi, you know intertwined souls have to work out their karma sometimes." Destinee shook her head. "Destiny fulfills itself if people only let fate take over. You of all people should know that. That's why you have to go to your reunion."

"The reunion." Jessi shuddered. "Why don't you tell me why Becky getting married has anything to do with me attending a weekend-long reunion of people I hated in high school accompanied by a boyfriend who doesn't exist."

Destinee rolled her eyes. "Oh, Jessi, it's so simple. Your mother wanted to know if you'd received your invitation to the reunion, and I said you weren't going to go, and she said she was so disappointed, but she supposed it was because you didn't have a man to bring and it didn't look like you ever would, so I sort of made up this really great boyfriend for you, and then she said you had to come to the reunion because it's the same weekend as your cousin's wedding to Tim and you work too hard, so you should take a vacation and everyone could meet him all at once."

Jessi leaned back in her chair and pinched the bridge of her nose. Destinee could cram more words into one sentence than most people used for a whole conversation.

Sighing, she said, "Okay. Let's go through this again. Slowly. My mother called."

Destinee nodded.

"Becky's getting married."

"Right."

"Let me guess what happened next. Mom got in one of her wistful moods, going on and on about she wants grandkids. How all she wants is to see me married before she dies. Are we still together here?"

Destinee nodded again. "I could tell by her voice her aura was gray, and the best way I knew to lighten it was to give her hope. I told her you'd met someone new, and she said you had to bring him along to meet the relatives. I mean, what else could I do?"

Jessi leaned back in her chair and closed her eyes, burying her hands into the thick locks at the crown of her head. Even as a little girl, that's how she'd reacted in moments of crisis, with her eyes closed, hugging her head. This was without question a crisis of major proportions. While she sat here, listening to Destinee's mumbo-jumbo, her mother was baking pies and making up the guest room for a nonexistent beau. Probably pricing wedding gowns, too. Maybe even baby layettes.

"Oh, honey, you need a connection. Here take some of my energy." Destinee ran behind the desk and grabbed Jessi in a huge bear hug. "Your glow is nearly gone. You simply have to have more confidence in the universe. You're a good person, so good things will happen to you. Don't forget that."

Jessi, never a touchy-feely person, endured the hug even though she was sure she'd be stabbed on her assistant's huge pointed-wing fairy lapel pin and end up bleeding to death on her desk. Although that might not be such a bad thing. The reunion was only three weeks away, and Becky's wedding the day after that.

The other alternative was to find a plausible fiancé to take home to meet her mother, the human lie detector, and then spend a week of hell trying to fool the people who'd known her all her life into believing she was in love. Oh yeah, and endure a reunion where she'd have to look at pictures of other people's kids and guess who people were from their name tags.

She wiggled away from Destinee, narrowed her eyes and studied her secretary with suspicion. Something was really wrong here. Things were never this straightforward with her mother or Destinee.

"Why do I have the feeling you still haven't told me everything?"

"Just one more little thing," Destinee replied, holding up her thumb and forefinger, indicating how tiny that thing was. "I told your mom to go ahead and tell Becky you'd be glad to be her maid of honor. Your dress will be ready when you get there."

Jessi's mouth dropped open and she gasped. She was going to appear in public in a dress Becky had picked out? She loved her cousin but abhorred her taste in clothing. Becky adored bright-printed flared skirts and with lacy blouses and flouncy dresses. Even hot pink was too conservative for her sometimes. Jessi didn't have to see the dress to know it would be some cotton candy confection, with a gazillion layers of organdy, big poofy sleeves and a huge bow on the butt. She groaned then resolved to put that particular problem aside to worry about later. She had more important things to take care at this moment.

Like her supposed new love. The one her mother was already cleaning the house for.

"Where do you propose I get this boyfriend you promised Mom?" Her voice radiated a calm she didn't feel. She couldn't take another hug.

"Rod in the medical benefits office next door is really nice," Destinee said with a note of hope. "He's wanted to go out with you for a long time."

"Rod is fifteen years older than me, has already had his eyes done twice and wears a bad toupee." Jessi held up her fingers and began ticking off all the other eligible men she knew before her assistant could. "Don from the accountant's office above us has three ex-wives and six children, so don't even go there. The guy who moved in to the place next to mine has had a different woman at his house every night for the last two months. I'm not desperate enough to hit the bars looking for a guy, or brave enough to sign up with an online service. You got any other ideas?"

Destinee brightened. "My sister's husband's brother. You know the tarot cards showed a possibility for love between you two and he's unattached again, but you won't even meet him."

Jessi held up her hand. "Stop right there. I don't even have to see him to know that won't work. Now call me picky if you'd like, but I don't think I have much in common with a guy in mirrored sunglasses and a camouflage cap. I'm sure he's a great guy, but I'm not into professional wrestling and I doubt if he'd care much for Bach and Vivaldi.

"Besides, according to you he changes girlfriends as often as most men change shirts. If I'm going to have to come up with a man, I prefer it be someone who won't leave me stranded at Becky's reception because he ran into a gorgeous blond with big boobs."

"You could hire a man for the weekend," Destinee said, tapping a fingernail against her teeth.

"There's that modeling agency two doors down. They probably have a guy you'd like. I'll bet there's enough money in the office supply budget to cover the fee."

"Enough, already!" Jessi walked into the bathroom and slammed the door. She could hear Destinee on the other side yelling out possible suitors and solutions until she turned on the water to drown out that insistent voice.

She was already in one big mess, thanks to Destinee, and she wasn't about to compound it by dating her secretary's redneck semi-relative or some guy from an actor's agency. It hadn't been that long since she'd been out with a man...well, okay, it had been that long, but she still wasn't desperate enough to pay someone. Yet.

She sat on the closed toilet seat and tried to figure out a sensible option, oblivious to Destinee's raps and shouted inquiries as to whether she was all right. There had to be a way out of this mess, just had to be. But short of hiring someone to kidnap her at the critical moment, she couldn't think of anything.

When her mind started running in circles, she gave up. She'd think about it at home. She had too much waiting for her here including a desk covered with a stack of paperwork, a pile of unanswered mail and several files she needed to study before morning. Any fantasies she'd harbored about home, hearth and Mr. Right had long been murdered by reality.

Back when she'd been an administrative assistant at an oil company, she'd dreamed of having her own business. It would give her independence, she'd thought, and make her rich. Richer anyway. Yet now she was more beholden to her clients than she ever had been to a boss and keeping the cash flow rolling was all on her. She'd made a success of her career, but as she'd been so vividly reminded this morning, she'd given up everything else in her life for it, including a love life.

It wasn't for a lack of opportunities. No, it was quite the contrary. She was the queen of first dates but a pauper when it came to second ones. Plenty of offers to dinner or a movie had come her way, nearly all of which she'd accepted. Still, nice as the men had been, there hadn't been a spark, at least not one that might become a full-blown blaze. The warm glow of affection was all she could imagine with any of them, never the hot flame of passion. Since most of those possibilities had come with an ex-wife, needy mother or host of children, she'd pretty much given up on finding even Mr. Not-Too-Bad.

Sighing, she stood, fluffed her hair in the mirror and unlocked the door. Destinee was sitting on Jessi's desk, eyes closed, humming a tuneless tone as she concentrated on the purple crystals she held in her loosely-closed fists.

"I'd like my desk back now," Jessi said in a soft, gentle tone.

Eyes closed, Destinee continued her humming, turning up the volume as she squinched her eyes even more tightly shut.

Jessi tried again. "I really need to get some work done." She stepped closer, until she was almost breathing into the other woman's ear. "So do you. NOW!"

Destinee's eyelids fluttered open, her humming ceased and her fists unclenched. She gave Jessi a radiant smile and jumped down, offering no explanation as to why she'd been up there in the first place.

"Early lunch, boss lady," she announced as she walked back to her own desk. "I'll be back in an hour or so."

"It's only 10 o'clock," Jessi called after her. "Couldn't you at least wait until you get the Cavett files done?"

Too late. Destinee had picked up her navy tote bag with its sun-and-moon design and disappeared. Sighing, Jessi headed to Destinee's desk to forward incoming calls to her own office.

She tried not to look at all the clutter but as usual was fascinated by Destinee's collection. A tiny gargoyle peeked over the top of the computer, a bright clock with fairies and flowers keeping time next to it. Crystals dangled from her standing files; a thin vial of some amber liquid marked her place in a sheaf of papers awaiting copying. But what really caught Jessi's eye was a clipped newspaper ad about a psychic fair going on at the park. Destinee had circled several booths, including an aura photographer, some psychic, and a Madame Broulee who promised to make your dreams come true overnight.

"Sorry, forgot something." Destinee popped in, grabbed the ad and took off out the door again with a wave of her hand. "I need that dollar-off coupon. I'm getting my aura read. It feels too chartreuse to me today."

The shrill of the phone reminded Jessi that, unlike her assistant, she'd have no lunch break. She had a stack of work to catch up on, the inevitable result of being away for several days. As an image consultant, she was expected to turn sow's ears into silk purses which seemed to require more effort all the time. She'd spent the last three days showing young mid-management executives business etiquette, dinner manners and the meaning of "office casual" dress. She'd decided there were no men and few women who knew the basics of polite society anymore. She'd like to blame it all on the entertainment industry, but she had feeling TV dinners and microwave pizzas had more to do with it. Who cared about a salad forks or water goblets when meals were burgers and fries from a bag?

Engrossed in her work, Jessi was surprised at how much time had passed before Destinee walked back in, looking like the cat who had swallowed the canary. She frowned. That look meant something wholly inappropriate for a place of business had happened or was about to. Jessi would never forget the time Destinee had told their most important client his inner spirit was polluted and started chanting some ancient Tibetan incantation over him. Luckily, he'd taken it in good humor. In fact, he had even asked Destinee to come to lunch and chant for his wife.

"What?" Jessi glared at Destinee, whose only response was to grin and start keyboarding. "You're got something up your sleeve, don't you?"

"Nope." Destinee pulled open her desk drawer and rooted for a granola bar. "I'm just looking forward to typing your report on the meeting with the Magellan Corporation and filing those Cavett documents."

"You have something to do first," Jessi reminded her. "Draft a letter to the reunion committee telling them I'm in a coma. Or dead. Backpacking in Siberia. You got me into this so get me out. Or find me a respectable man."

She smiled wanly. "Considering that my last date took me to see the decorated Christmas trees at the art museum, I guess you better start writing. After all, that was what, seven months ago?"

Destinee's smile widened as she picked up a file but she didn't speak. Disconcerted by her secretary's sudden and most unusual reluctance to talk, Jessi went back to the slowly diminishing pile of correspondence and phone messages on her desk, curiosity fading into the routine of business. She didn't even realize how late it was until Destinee stood in front of her, bidding her goodnight.

"Remember," the secretary said, her tone grave, "our fates are writ upon the stars, and we have no choice but to accept what destiny holds." Then she giggled and wiggled her fingers in farewell. "Gotta run; I've got a pizza coming and I have to get home before it gets there. I hope that cute guy brings it again."

"Did you write the letter?" Jessi called after her but to no avail. Destinee had already disappeared out the door.

****

She was back in the office before Jessi the next morning, breathing in the heavy scent of sage leaves smoldering in a brass burner atop the file cabinet. Jessi choked out a greeting and shut the door between the two offices, hoping the leaves would burn out in a hurry. Destinee swore it was an Indian rite of purification, but Jessi suspected it was her way to keep customers from showing up too early in the morning.

Jessi hadn't been at her desk long before a knock came at her door. She yelled "Come in" without looking up. Instead of Destinee, a delivery boy with a breathtaking arrangement of cut flowers stood in front of her. She fumbled in her purse, found some bills for a tip and set the bouquet on a low table beneath her window.

The arrangement was beautiful and looked expensive. She was sure who sent them. It had to be the CEO of the company who'd hired her to train his executives last week. Still, she untied the card and slipped it from the envelope.

She frowned and looked at the envelope again. Her name was definitely there, but the shop had stuck the wrong card inside. She opened the dividing door, handed the card to Destinee and instructed her to call the florist shop to see who the flowers were meant to go to. Moments later Destinee walked back and said, "They're yours. The guy came in this morning, paid cash and didn't give his name. Enjoy."

Jessi stared at her, perplexed, tapping the card on the table. There had to be a mix-up. "You expect me to believe this message is meant for me?"

"No question about it, boss lady." Jessi noticed a

glow in Destinee's eyes and a flush to her cheeks.

"What do you know about this?" she demanded in suspicion. "'Fess up, or you're fired."

"I didn't have anything to do with it. Really. Although I'm so excited that you have a secret admirer, and obviously your karmas have intersected. This is so cool; the fates have driven him to take action at the exact time you needed him."

Jessi waved her out and reread the card. She traced the bold strokes with her finger as she read the few words: "The minutes are like hours when we're apart. Only six more days, my darling."

The signature read "Damian."

She didn't know a Damian. Never had. He sounded like someone Destinee would know...

Destinee. What had it said in that ad she'd grabbed and taken with her? Something about some spell-caster who promised to make dreams come true overnight.

****

Jessi tucked the card into her purse with a stern mental reminder that no one could conjure up a man. The arrival of these flowers the day after Destinee had gone to that psychic fair was a coincidence, that's all. They had to be from someone she knew who was setting her up for a practical joke. Becky maybe. Her cousin would never believe Jessi had a serious boyfriend and kept it from her.

Jessi took the flowers home to her condo, telling herself they'd brighten the place up. The place was a rental she'd been in for several years. She intended to buy a house as soon as she found the right house, which would be easier if it didn't take so long to check them out. The bright blooms added color to the beige walls and brown carpet were standard in every room but the all-white kitchen. Her eyes kept returning to those flowers. They reminded her how neutral her life had become, just like her home. Her working wardrobe was tailored suits or khakis and a company polo; her off-work wardrobe was mostly pajamas. Most nights she got home so late there was little reason to change into anything else.

She split the hour between eating supper and going to bed watching a cop drama on TV as she checked her e-mail and social media to see if she'd missed anything. She was about to log off when on impulse, she typed in the name of a popular dating site. A half hour passed as she clicked onto various profiles and debated whether she was willing to put her own picture and profile out there for everyone to see.

"No." Jessi hit the sleep key. "I'm not that desperate yet,"

Maybe, but she was talking to herself. She was pretty sure carrying on one-sided conversations was a sign of impending old maidhood.

Her bed felt like a soft embrace when she slipped between the sheets after falling asleep on the couch. The stress of catching up at work plus worrying about some anonymous admirer was exhausting. She'd made sure the door was both locked and dead bolted just in case. She watched those TV true crime shows and would not become the subject of one. With her luck, her mother would give the crew that stupid senior prom picture she loved and Jessi detested. She turned over, folded the pillow under head and went to sleep to the sound of rain against the window.

Weariness swept across her. She was in the great hall, keeping an eye on the servants who were preparing it for the upcoming reunion. Her father had sent a courier to tell them he'd be home within the fortnight. She intended to have everything in place for a huge celebration when he and his warriors arrived, no matter how hard she and her servants had to work.

"A messenger." The words came from a breathless lad who'd run in across the fresh-swept floors. Rather than scold him, she sent him to the kitchen with instructions for the cook to give him an apple and took off the tunic that covered her dress. She smoothed her hair and walked to the courtyard to see what needed to be done.

A thrill of recognition ran through her as the tall man turned and bowed. He'd come again, this courtier who had so caught her fancy. She stood just inside the opened wooden door, out of the rain. The newcomer refused her offer to step inside.

"I would not soil your floors with my boots," he said, adjusting the hood of his clock to keep the moisture from striking his face. "I have come to speak to the lord of this castle; I have a message from the duke."

"My father is away." Her voice was strong. "I supervise the hold in his absence."

"My message is only for the lord."

She nodded. Such was the world. Men ruled and women obeyed, especially those perceived to be young and inexperienced. Even the arrival of the leader of the guards, who stayed behind to defend the keep and those who lived here, could not dissuade him from his mission.

As the two men spoke, she studied the new arrival. His blasted hood kept her from seeing more than the curve of his scarred cheek and the slope of his narrow nose. She longed to see his eyes. They were, as her father often reminded her, the window into one's soul.

Arms wrapped around herself, she wondered why this man had such an attraction for her. She would soon marry, she knew; her father had hinted he was already looking at alliances. Yet she could not imagine herself sharing a bed with any of the men most suitable.

This man…he brought strange feelings inside her, a sense of kinship. She would not resist his arms around her or his lips seeking a kiss. She fought the desire to lean toward him and tip her face to him.

Beep…beep…beep…

Jessi slammed the off button and fell back against her pillow. Why couldn't she have this dream on the weekend when she didn't have to get up? She closed her eyes and tried to recapture the fading images but to no avail. Sighing, she got up to face the day. She had enough to worry about in the real world without borrowing mysteries from her imagination.

Chapter Two

Jessi had been at the office less than an hour when the new gift came. This time the note in the now-familiar writing read, "Nothing is as sweet as you; this is the closest I could find. D."

Small things had been arriving every day for two weeks. She'd given up questioning their origins. She'd also given up fighting a return to Michigan. Destinee was adamant that Jessi's fate lay in Durkin and enlisted Jessi's mother in the battle. Some forces are too strong to fight, like the combination of the fates and Molly Flint. Bowing to the inevitable, she bought a gray summer suit, a plane ticket and a bagful of lotions the sales clerk swore would make her look ten years younger.

She'd even managed to tolerate her assistant's intense lectures about trusting in the fates instead of the rules society had imposed on her.

"Fate has a plan for each of us." Destinee's eyes glowed with sincerity. "Souls entwine without our knowledge, driven by eternity. Embrace the gifts that are bestowed upon you."

Jessi had smiled and nodded, her fallback at times like this. She lived her life by logic and the rules of society Destinee tended to flaunt. The story of lovers spanning time and planes of existence made for great movies but that's all it was, pure fiction.

The final gift arrived just before she left for the airport and her flight to Michigan. She waited until she was sitting at the gate before she opened the box. A small silver locket on a fine chain was accompanied by a longer note from her secret admirer, telling her how much he longed to hold her in his arms. She fastened it around her neck despite her reservations. It would be such a shame for it to languish ignored. After all, she reminded herself, there was no way to send it back to a man who didn't exist - or if he did, had been summoned up in a tent at a park, like in a scene from the old "Twilight Zone" series. She wouldn't be surprised to see Rod Serling popping in any minute to offer an introduction to tonight's series. Sure, he was dead, but her supposed adoring boyfriend didn't exist either.

Her mantra throughout the trip was, "This is nuts," the sentiment that popped in her head every time she thought about the stupidity of what she was doing. She'd hated high school and longed for the day when she could escape Durkin. She could see herself all alone at the reunion, a perfect target for long and boring stories about little Johnny's potty training and his sister Susie's incredible musical ability from all her former classmates. Then the next day, she'd be the pity of the relatives, enduring their questions about why she hadn't made that walk down the aisle yet.

She touched the locket. The time on the plane next to her sleeping seatmate had given her time away from it all to organize her thoughts. Destinee had sent the gifts, of course. By the time Jessi landed, her assistant would have called Mom and explained that Mr. Right had been tied up in a business deal and couldn't make it. Her mother would convince everyone else and voila! Mom saved face with the relatives and after she got home, Jessi could make up the gory details of a break-up.

She might even be able to parlay her imaginary man into an excuse to make appearances and take off in ten minutes. A marvelous thought struck her. She might even be able to make Becky believe it would be bad luck to be in her wedding and save her from the dress disaster of the century.

****

A smile broke across Jessi's face as she neared the luggage area and spotted her mother, the indomitable Molly Flint, with a welcome home sign. Sometimes the woman drove her nuts, especially since her father died and she was the sole focus of her mom's attention, but she loved her dearly.

"Darling, you look wonderful."

The sign fell to the floor as Molly pulled her into a tight hug. Linking her arm with Jessi's, she led the way to the baggage carousel.

"How was your flight?" her mother asked.

"Smooth. Boring."

"That's because you were in a hurry to get here."

Her mother's grin and dancing eyes put Jessi on the alert. Something was definitely up.

"You know I love coming home."

"It's too late for your surprise." Molly gave a little shake of excitement. "His plane was early and we've already met."

"Met who?"

"Your Damian, silly. He's right over there getting a rental car."

"Damian?" Jessi echoed, turning to look behind her. A tall figure stood at the counter, a single bag sitting by his feet. When he turned and waved, she felt obliged to wave back.

"What a marvelously romantic name," her mother sighed. "Damian St. Clair. There's something so, well, old-fashioned about it. And if a man ever looked like his name...well, I don't have to tell you, do I?" She sighed again, then added, "He told me you wanted to introduce him to me yourself, but honey, he was so excited when he called my cell phone. I can tell he loves you very much. And that voice - oh, my! It made even my old heart flutter."

Jessi braced herself as the man picked up his bag and started toward them. She couldn't believe she was about to meet the man who'd sent her gift after gift, her supposed boyfriend in all his glory. And glory was pretty close to a perfect description. Tall, dark and handsome didn't begin to cover things. A black suit fit his wide-shouldered, lean body to perfection and his tanned face was golden against his crisp white shirt.

Page 35

Her luggage was forgotten as long, fast steps brought him to her. His arms reached toward her, his deep voice filling with delight as he said, "Oh, Jessi darling, I've missed you!"

Then she was wrapped against him, tight to his broad chest as he embraced her. The soft silk of his shirt whispered against her skin as he held her close, his breath warm against her hair as he enveloped her in a lover's hold. The contours of his body felt natural and familiar; it was as if she'd done this a million times before. Yet she was acutely aware of the brisk scent of his aftershave, the coarseness of the stubble that grazed her cheek, the strength in the arms and the unmistakable huskiness of his voice as he said "I'd love to say hello you properly, but your mother is watching." He gave her a chaste kiss and loosened the embrace, stepping away to grab her bags as they moved along the carousel.

"He's dreamy," her mother whispered as Damian returned, carrying her heavy suitcases as if they were pillows and not fifty pounds of clothes, shoes and all that anti-aging, skin-tightening make-up the saleslady had assured her would take years off her face. When he smiled, a shiver of recognition shimmied down Jessi's spine.

He was the man from her dreams. No wonder he'd looked so familiar, from the green flecks in his deep brown eyes to the slightly jagged scar along his jaw line. He was the man of her dreams. Same height. Same handsome features, same warrior's body.

She felt a blush rise in her cheeks as she remembered the sort of things she'd fantasized about doing with the tall, handsome man in her dreams. The man who stood before her seemed to remember that intimacy as well.

But he couldn't be. Not even Destinee could have pulled that one off. No one knew. The dreams had been so precious, so incredibly real, that she'd never told another living soul about them.

A chill snaked through her as Damian slid an arm around her waist and pulled her close. Who was this man? Where had he come from?

How could a stranger be so perfectly, completely right?

"Jessi?" Her mother's frustrated voice penetrated the fog. "You must be jet-lagged, dear. Didn't you hear me? I wanted to know if you were hungry. We could eat at that cute little diner just outside the airport, or we could wait till we get home."

"Home," Jessi answered without hesitation. The last thing she needed was to sit in a diner booth beside her imaginary lover come to life, his thigh against hers, his hand reaching out to brush back her hair or offer her a bite of his sandwich. She needed time to figure out what was going on here and enough breathing room to pull herself back together. Her mother might not be the most observant woman in the world, but even she would figure out before long that there was something wrong with her little girl.

"How about you, Damian? Do you mind waiting?" Molly turned to her daughter's boyfriend. "Or have you eaten already?"

"Just peanuts on the plane, but I vote with Jessi. From what she's said about your cooking, a seven-course meal in a five-star restaurant can't compare to one of your dinners. Especially your chocolate cream pie and the fried chicken you make for the church suppers."

A cold chill shook Jessi. There was no way Damian could know how much she raved about her mother's cooking skills, or that she never ate any chocolate pie but her mother's.

What if he really was an all-knowing creature created through some sort of spell? Shouldn't she have some kind of counter-spell just in case things got a little too intense?

"How did you know about the pie?" She hissed under her breath as her mother led the out of the terminal.

"As many times as you've raved about it?" Damian lifted an eyebrow in surprise. "How could I not know?"

Jessi felt another shiver. She had never believed in magic, UFOs or psychic phenomenon. She was a realist. She only believed in what she could prove, which meant this was someone's idea of a practical joke. This guy, whoever it was, had been coached by someone who knew her well. That's all it was. She was determined to find out who it was before her vacation was over, or die trying.

Her friend Heather, maybe? They'd been best buds since grade school, and Heather knew she was flying solo. Heaven knows, they'd talked about it enough during their keep-in-touch phone calls. Or maybe Becky had arranged it. She of all people should know better than to even suggest a blind date to Jessi. But women in love seemed to have a driving need to make sure everyone else was hooked up, too.

"You two kids can ride to the house together," Molly said as Damian loaded their suitcases into the trunk. "I'm sure you have lots to talk about." Then, to Jessi's amazement, she winked.

"No, no," Jessi protested. "I need to know what the schedule is this week. He can follow us."

Her mother hesitated and for a moment Jessi had visions of being shoved into a luxury sedan with a stranger while her mother blithely drove away, completely oblivious to the danger her oldest child might be in. Damian's added "She's right, you two need to catch up," tipped the scales in Jessi's favor. Walking into the parking garage, sliding into her mother's car and reaching the exit at ground level took about ten minutes. She so hoped that there would be no black rental with Damian behind the wheel when they rolled out onto the exit drive. But there he was, big as life, falling in right behind them.

To her relief, her mother talked about the

upcoming shower, wedding and reception during the short drive home, which meant Jessi didn't have to talk. That was a good thing because she couldn't have carried on a conversation right now, not with Damian's image dancing through her brain.

Someone had gone to great lengths to set up a practical joke, and she intended to find out who it was before things went too far. It couldn't have been Destinee, she knew. That girl didn't have a dishonest bone in her body. The few friends she saw regularly back home were more like social acquaintances, without the knowledge or inclination to do something like this.

Heather or Becky. It had to be one or the other. Or maybe both. They knew she was perfectly happy being manless, and would refused any attempt at yet another fix-up, so this was probably their underhanded way to do just that.

"Ah, home sweet home." Molly slowed and pulled into the driveway of a white two-story frame house and cut the engine. Jessi was out of the car as soon as it stopped, before Damian could get out and open the door for her. She needed space. She needed to be alone, to sort out the impossible. To immerse herself in the familiar until she could get her bearings.

"Your mom's great." Damian whispered to her as they walked down the front sidewalk. "You're not mad that I spoiled the surprise, though, are you?"

The shimmer of light from a streetlight fell across his face, and on it she saw the same seductive smile that she'd seen only hours before, bestowed on her by a king's messenger in the same dream castle that had filled her sleep off and on for fifteen years. Tension coiled inside her.

Good heavens, could this be Destinee's handiwork after all? Had she consulted a witch at that psychic fair, someone who actually could create a man from a wish?

She didn't have time to stew over it. Her mother settled Damian in the family room in front of the evening news while she dragged Jessi to the kitchen. Ostensibly, she needed help getting the roast out of the oven and the fresh-baked bread sliced. Jessi knew better, though. She knew her mother planned to weasel out any information she could about Damian.

"Damian seems nice." The innocuous remark was loaded with unasked questions, which Jessi intended to leave that way. "I thought we'd watch a movie and then I'll skedaddle so you two can be alone. Damian said you haven't seen each other for several weeks."

"We've been busy." At least Jessi had. She had no idea what fantasy men did when they weren't being, well, fantastic. "I'll bet Becky's been even busier, trying to put together a wedding in such a short time. I don't suppose you know any of the details, do you?"

As Molly rattled on about Becky's trouble finding the perfect dress and the difficulty of finding a good photographer on short notice, Jessi grabbed a knife and began slicing the loaf of homemade bread her mother had left on the counter. There was a comfort in being back in the kitchen where she'd helped cook so many meals, back in the house that had barely changed since she'd left for college fifteen years before.

She sensed Damian as he came into the kitchen and leaned against the doorway. She felt his eyes watching her and it took everything she had to just keep chopping, as if they were an established couple, used to the presence of each other.

"Dining room or kitchen?" Molly asked.

"Dining room."

"Kitchen."

When Jessi and Damian spoke at the same time, Molly laughed. "You two sound like Jessi's father and me," she said. "I've always liked eating in the dining room, and he preferred the kitchen table. Since Damian's our guest, we'll eat in here."

Jessi wanted to grab the plates and silverware and rush everyone to the dining room, where three people around a table made for eight would put plenty of space between her and Damian. Yet five minutes later, they were sitting down together in the intimate atmosphere of the kitchen, with only the ridiculously narrow space of the table separating her from her supposed boyfriend.

Molly chattered all through the meal like always, filling Jessi in on all the town gossip and not even noticing she hardly spoke. Finally, to Jessi's relief, the meal was finished.

A moment later, she wished it had lasted longer. She'd been home less than an hour and her mother was delivering a lecture.

"I'm sure you're a fine man," Molly told

Damian, "or my girl wouldn't have chosen you. But I am a bit old-fashioned so I hope you'll respect that. What you two do as consenting adults in your homes is your business. But I expect you to be modest in mine." She took a deep breath. "So I'd appreciate it if you'd use the guest room during your stay while Jessi sleeps in hers. I do hope you'll understand."

Jessi admired the way Damian reassured her red-faced mother. Not, of course, that he had a chance in hell of sharing her bed. She might be impulsive at times and he might be sex incarnate but she wasn't about to sleep with a man she'd met only hours before even if he did make her innards do flips. Shoot, she didn't even know if he was real or, like Cinderella's coachman, would turn into a mouse at the stroke of midnight. She wouldn't be the least surprised if all there was of him in the morning was a sprinkle of shimmer where he'd slept.

She grabbed her suitcases before Damian could get them and lugged them up the open stairs to the second floor. Dumping them in her room, she offered him a choice of the other two guest rooms, showed him the bathroom and advised him where the linens were kept. When he took his own carry-on into the room across from hers, she followed him in and sat down on the bed.

"Out with it." She watched as he began to unpack the case that she was certain was real leather, not a knock-off like hers. The clothes he lifted out, already on hangers, were fashion-magazine quality and his shoes probably cost more than her entire wardrobe. Whoever conjured him had done a fine job with his accessories as well.

Or whoever had hired him, which was so much likelier.

"What do you mean?" Damian asked, a slight frown creasing his forehead.

"We've never met before. We are not in love and discussing wedding plans. You do not know my favorite movie, the comfort food I'd kill for or my biggest phobia."

"Anything with Brad Pitt, mashed potatoes with white gravy and big, nasty spiders." Damian zipped the empty bag shut and tucked it in the closet beneath the neat line of his clothes. He turned to her with a smile. "How could I not know those?"

"Stop it!" Jessi jumped off the bed to confront

him. "You're good, I'll give you that. But let's cut through the crap. Who are you and who put you up to this?"

He reached out to stroke her hair, his eyes dancing. "I wish you'd told me ahead of time about your fantasy. We could have started this whole thing at the airport. Strangers accidentally meeting, drawn to each other in an instant…not that it's too late to start now."

Jessi stepped back to put space between them. Things had been crazy with her business lately and maybe she'd finally cracked. Could be she was tucked into a nice bed in a psych ward, stoned on really good drugs, while her mind created this imaginary world. She crossed her arms and studied Damian.

Either he was right, they were lovers and she'd forgotten it all in some fugue state. Or she was right and either, A, Destinee's witchy friends had made him of thin air or, B, she was living in la-la land right now. Did it really matter? Why not play it out and see what happened next?

"I'm sorry." She moved to him and wrapped her arms around his neck. "I should have told you. Are you mad at me?"

Damian smiled down at her. "Like I could ever be. Can I have one kiss before we go back to not knowing each other?"

She raised her face to him in invitation. His lips were warm and firm as they met hers, the kiss deepening until she was on her toes, fingers buried in his thick hair with wild yet familiar excitement running through her body. Disappointment filled her when he broke their kiss and moved away.

"Promise me we'll get acquainted really fast, okay?" The rasp in his voice assured her he'd felt the same need. She nodded, too unsure of herself to speak. This thing might only last until Becky's wedding was over but she intended to take advantage of every second she had with this man.

"Like we've known each other forever," she finally said.

A shadow moved over Damian's face.

"Forever." His fingers stroked her cheek. "Linked for eternity."

Chapter Three

"I've made popcorn, kids." Her mother's no-nonsense shout was like a cold wave, reminding Jessi they were not alone. She knew if they didn't go down right away, her mother would be up to check on them. That's just how Mom was.

"Hey." Damian stopped her as she started for the door. "Just relax and have a good time. That's why we are here."

Jessi ran down the steps ahead of him. Her mother's voice stopped her as she headed for the kitchen to grab some cans of pop.

"I've got it all in here, honey." Jessi walked into the living room. Her mother had two bowls of popcorn on the coffee table, one large and one small, and a half-dozen cans of cola on a tray. A clear jar held chocolate-shelled candies and an unopened bag of Jessi's favorite treat, red licorice twists, lay beside it. Her mother had gone all out. Either she was really tired of watching movies alone or she was trying to impress Damian. Or both.

"You kids can have the couch." Molly waited until Jessi sat and her friend took his place beside her to hand over the big bowl of popcorn. Telling them to wait a moment, she ran into the kitchen and came back with three tumblers filled with ice.

"I don't want you to think we're not civilized." She gave Damian a quick smile. "Now do you prefer the diet kind or the real stuff?"

Once they'd all settled with their snacks, Molly pushed the DVR button and let the movie begin. Having Jessi home felt so right; having her boyfriend here as well made her nearly ecstatic. She was proud of everything her daughter had accomplished but she didn't want Jessi's drive to keep her from having everything that life offered.

Had she been to fault? She'd wondered that more than once. With only one chick to brood over, maybe she'd pushed too hard. Ralph, rest his soul, had told her from time to time that she should lighten up a little. But Jessi had always been her daddy's little girl; Molly had dismissed Ralph's tendency to spoil her. She had expected Jessi to get her college degree, find a job, meet the right man and live the same sort of small town life as all of her friends. Jessi's drive had pushed down a different path, though, leaving her still single at thirty-one.

Not for long, however, if Molly had anything to do with it. Those two needed to spend more alone time if their relationship was going to end at the altar. And while they were here, she intended to make sure they had all they needed.

The recliner was the perfect place to watch the two of them. While they got lost in the movie, she relished the sight of Jessi leaning against Damian. His arm was dropped around her shoulders as if he needed contact with her. Molly remembered that feeling. She and Ralph had loved each other right up to his death three years ago. Some of her friends grew away from their spouses, but not her. There was no one's company she had enjoyed more than Ralph's or anyone she'd rather spend time with.

Now all she had were memories of how it felt to be the center of someone's world. She was at peace with Ralph's passing from a major heart attack, although she'd felt at first that she should have died with him.

Page 51

Watching Jessi and Damian reminded her how much life still held.

Like wedding plans and, hallelujah, grandchildren at last.

****

Jessi woke to bright sunlight. She glanced at the bedside alarm clock. After nine and she didn't hear a single sound from across the hall. Either Damian was an early riser or he dissipated into whatever made-up men became after the sun set. She tossed the covers back, slid her feet into her slippers and took a deep breath.

Time to face the truth.

Gripping the doorknob with slightly shaky fingers, she gave it a turn and pushed the door open. As she expected, the bed was empty. She walked cautiously to the mussed sheets and looked for dust or other evidence that her new boyfriend had crumbled into nothingness.

"You're supposed to come to my bed while I'm still in it."

Jessi whirled to face an amused Damian wearing nothing but one of her mother's burgundy bath towels around his waist. She hoped he didn't expect an answer because the sight took her breath away. Wide shoulders, well-muscled chest, and muscular arms that make women remember the definition of "swoon." Granted, she wasn't the world's foremost expert on naked men but she was pretty sure he'd rank in the top ten. Top three, even.

He walked past her, headed for the closet and clothes. She caught a whiff of soap and some sort of musky aftershave. The combination was sexy. Sexy enough, in fact, that Jessi decided it was time to retreat before she did something she'd regret. Like yank off that towel and shove him onto the bed to have her way with him.

"Gotta get dressed," she mumbled as she took back off across the hall. She'd planned to put on at-home clothes, shorts and a tee, but instead she found herself examining the clothes she'd brought. Settling on khaki capris and a hot pink tank top, she used the curling rod on her hair instead of pulling it back into a ponytail and even added a little blush and earrings to her look.

"My, you look nice," her mother said as she walked into the kitchen. "Doesn't she, Damian?"

"She always looks good." He winked at Jessi. "I

figure she got her fashion sense from her mother."

"Oh, you." A flush of color brightened Molly's cheeks. "You're quite the charmer, aren't you?"

She turned around and pulled a baking sheet from the oven. The smell of homemade biscuits filled the air; Jessi was suddenly ravenous. When her mother set them on the table and then brought over sausage gravy, scrambled eggs and fried potatoes, she was done for. She realized her usual routine breakfast of yogurt and berries was history as long as she was here in Durkin. In fact, she suspected her entire pattern of eating healthy and taking a daily walk was going to be suspended.

She bowed her head while her mother offered a blessing and managed to be polite enough to wait until the biscuits were passed before grabbing one and taking a bite. The buttery treat melted in her mouth and reminded her what a great cook her mother was. She probably ought to copy her recipes or ask for culinary lessons but she knew she'd never have time to use the skill. Bags of salad fixing and pre-cooked grilled chicken give her a quick and easy meal at the end of a long day.

"Are you sure you want another biscuit, honey?"

Jessi knew the message between her mother's soft words which was "Should you eat like that in front of your man?" Mom was old school and believed that women should eat like birds around men and pig out in private. Jessi might have considered that if the circumstances were different. But Mr. Summoned Up beside her was going to love her no matter what. That was the beauty of magic.

"I love women with a good appetite." Damian leaned over and kissed a bit of jelly off the corner of her mouth.

Jessi almost giggled. She felt like a teenager with her first boyfriend again, that's how long it been since she'd been in a real relationship.

Her mother steered the conversation to questions about her guest. Jessi listened intently. She had to make sure they had their stories straight if they were going to pull this off for the next week.

"Tell me how you two met," Molly suggested. "My daughter has always been less than forthcoming about her boyfriends."

Jessi could translate that one pretty easy, too.

The hidden meaning was "I had no idea she was even dating anymore." She wondered how her mother would feel if she knew the truth about the man she'd welcomed into her house.

The story he told sounded plausible. They'd met at a local coffee shop when he'd accidentally picked up her order instead of his. When they kept running into each other there, he'd finally gotten the nerve to ask her out.

"I couldn't believe it when she said yes." Damian took Jessi's hand and held it loosely in his. "After the third date I decided maybe she was going out with me because she liked me and not from pity."

Dang, this guy was good. Jessi nodded and tried to say the right thing as Damian spun stories from their supposed shared life. The details were there. She did make frequent trips to the public library, was a near fanatic about the local college basketball team and indulged her weakness for ice cream at least once a week at the small café near her office.

But why wouldn't he know? Destinee's witchy woman would have made sure to conjure up the right memories, after all. Jessi wondered how much her assistant had spent. Whatever it was, she needed to reimburse her. Double, maybe even triple.

Her mother might have probed for information all day if two things hadn't happened: The doorbell rang and, instants later, her cousin Becky dropped into the empty chair to her and said, "You've been here how long and I haven't seen you yet?"

Before Jessi could answer, her cousin had leaned over and grabbed her in a tight hug. As soon as Becky released her, a second interrogation of Damian began. This time Jessi cut it off after a couple of questions. Enough was enough.

"You kids talk." Molly gathered the dishes and carried them to the sink. "I've got to run to the store or we'll be eating eggs again for supper. I wanted to learn Damian's likes before I stocked up on groceries."

Jessi and Becky exchanged amused glances. They both knew that when Molly got nervous, she went shopping. Having her daughter home, meeting Damian and helping with Becky's wedding was the trifecta of stress.

Damian excused himself to supposedly make business calls which left the two cousins alone. He'd no more than walked out the front door when Becky propped her head in her hands, elbows on the table, and said, "So give."

"What?" Jessi played stupid.

"Seriously. Not one single word about men or dating and you show up with that magnificent specimen of manhood. Anybody that gorgeous has to be fantastic in bed. He is, isn't he? Like porn star fantastic, right?"

Jessi held up a warning finger.

"Unless you'd like to give up every single detail about you and Tim, I'd suggest you stop the inquisition. The reason you didn't know about him is that everything has happened incredibly fast. One day I'm going along with life as usual and then bam! Damian drops in it and everything changed."

"Ooh." Becky grinned. "Did Prince Charming come on a white horse?"

Jessi laughed. "More like a white Maserati." The fun of make-believe was that she could say anything and get away with it.

"Dang. Dang. The man looks like that and he's rich, too. Remind me again why I'm marrying Tim instead of holding out for Prince Charming's brother."

"Because you adore Tim and he adores you. Forget about me. I want to hear every single detail of your wedding."

"He's going overseas for the next six months." Becky's face became solemn. "Mom still wants us to wait until he comes back to get married but we're going ahead and doing it now. I mean, if anything happens…"

"Don't even think about that. Concentrate on your big event."

"I know." Becky took a deep breath. "My apartment's way too small for the two of us so I'm going house hunting while he's gone. I figure it will take the whole time to get everything exactly as I want it when he walks in for the first time."

"First things first. Tell me you're wearing a traditional wedding dress and not a vampire costume or something."

A peal of laughter came in response. Becky was famous in the family for her wild fashion choices. Jessi deliberately didn't ask about her maid of honor dress. She needed another good night's sleep before she faced that.

****

"See you tomorrow." Becky hugged Jessi as she got ready to leave. "I'll pick you up about eleven and we'll go to the wedding shop."

The house was quiet after Becky left. Jessi relished the alone time. The last two days had been absolutely crazy. After all that time worrying how she was going to explain the lack of the promised fiancé, here he was sleeping right across the hall. Her big concern now was how she could keep up the charade long enough to survive both the reunion and the family grilling at Becky's reception.

Snapping on the radio fastened on the bottom of a kitchen cabinet, she ran hot water in the sink and poured in detergent from the bottle on the window sill. The combination of the music and the mundane task of washing dishes relaxed her. When arms closed around her and a voice whispered "Hello beautiful" in her ear, she jumped and gave a little scream. Damian stepped away; she whirled to face him, dish cloth clasped in her hands.

"Not the reaction I hoped for," he said with a smile.

"You scared me." Jessi dropped the cloth and

wiped her hands on the towel hanging from a chair back. "Did you get your calls made?"

"Actually I walked around town a little. It's a pretty place."

"Which is a pseudonym for boring. You can be honest."

"You've got everything you need here. Hardware, grocery store, beauty salon – what more can you want?"

"Let's start with a place that serves a decent cup of coffee and maybe a movie theater. I'd even settle for a chain hamburger place. Not that the bar doesn't have great food if you like everything fried, of course."

"Somehow I missed that. How about you show me around?"

Jessi hadn't planned on leaving the house any more than she had to. Durkin was one of those towns where news traveled fast and her bringing a man to meet her mother would be front and center on the gossip chain. Making their first joint appearance at the reunion was perfect. Introductions, a moment of chatting and then move on – in and out, quick and easy. The grapevine would spread the information and the flurry of interest would have died down by Becky's wedding the next day. But Damian was waiting for an answer. If it was "no," she knew he'd want an explanation and she was not about to go there. He apparently didn't realize he wasn't going to be around in the long run and she didn't intend to be the one who broke it to him.

"Give me a minute."

"We can do it later if you want," Damian said.

"Afternoons get really hot here in the summer. I'd rather go now while it's still comfortable outside."

Jessi found her walking shoes and slipped them on. She found Damian on the porch, stretched out on the rattan chaise with his eyes closed. She tiptoed over, put her hands over his eyes and said, "Guess who?"

"The Queen of England?"

"Try again," Jessi said with a laugh.

"Miss America?"

"Closer."

"How about the most beautiful woman in Durkin, Michigan?" Damian pulled her on top of him with one quick move.

"Flatterer."

"It's true." His eyes met hers. "You've always

been the most beautiful woman I've ever known and always will be."

Her face was only inches from his, close enough she could see the delicate scar along one temple and the tiny wrinkles at the corner of his eyes. Near for her to close the small distance between them and touch her lips to his in a tentative kiss. Damian wrapped his arms around her and deepened the kiss; his tongue slipped inside her open mouth to meet hers.

Jessi slid her fingers into his hair and gave into nearly forgotten sensations as his arms held her close and his mouth worked its magic. To hell with where he came from. Nothing that felt this right could be wrong.

Or be so noticeable, she realized when she heard her mother loudly clearing her throat. She scrambled off the chaise, and Damian. Her mother's small smile only made getting caught just that much worse.

"Let me take those," she said, grabbing for the grocery bags.

"I've got it." Her mother swung them out of range. "This is your vacation, remember?"

Of all the places Jessi might have chosen as her ideal relaxation destination, Durkin wasn't anywhere on the list. Actually, Michigan wasn't on there either. Her idea of a perfect getaway was a suite in a luxury hotel in some tropical paradise.

"We were about to explore the town." Damian took Jessi's hand in his. "She's promised to show me the seedy side of this place."

Molly gave them a "go on" wave, pulled the screen door open with her food and carried the groceries in. Jessi left her hand in Damian's as they headed down the steps and toward what passed for a downtown in Durkin.

"I believe you were about to buy me a beer," he said.

No, I was about to let you do anything you wanted right there on the porch.

"I hope they let me run a tab. I left my purse behind."

"Promise me you'll be a cheap date and I'll pay."

"Wow, I feel special," Jessi laughed.

Their light spirits continued as they strolled down the sidewalk. Jessi pointed out the local landmarks from the old Victorian rumored to have been a house of ill repute to the consignment store that used to be a video store.

"Before that it was a pizza place, I think, and I'm pretty sure it started out as a gas station."

"And you told me this place was boring," Damian teased.

"Wait till tonight," she said. "The city fathers roll up the sidewalks at six."

"So we'd better make the best of today."

They started at the small ice cream parlor that had opened since Jessi's last trip home. Torn between mint chocolate chip and very vanilla, she chose a scoop of each. Damian went a step further and ordered a banana split rich with syrup and topped with whipped cream and bright red cherries. They ate in a companionable silence until Damian pushed his metal boat away and said, "Enough."

Jessi laughed and scooped the last of her own ice cream into her mouth. Leaning back in her chair, feeling too full to move, she gave a deep sigh of satisfaction.

"Tell me what it was like growing up here," Damian suggested.

She shook her head. "Tell me a story from your past."

Page 65

"What do you want to know?"

"Anything. What you were like as a kid."

He laughed. "I was a geek. Comic book collection, button down shirts and all."

Jessi arched an eyebrow. That was hard to believe.

"I had two best friends from kindergarten through high school. Boy Scouts, chess club, the whole works."

"You're serious."

"Yeah." Damian gave her a crooked grin. "Does that mean you're going to dump me now?"

"Not until I get to know you a little better."

"That's right. I forgot. We're playing two strangers stranded in a small town."

"Something like that. Now tell me more about your nerd background. I'm fascinated."

"You're lying. But I'll indulge your wish, strange lady."

His recounting of his adventures with his friends had her laughing so hard at times that she could hardly breathe. He was such a good storyteller that she could almost see him in a robot costume made of aluminum foil and boxes on Halloween. When he began to talk about his high school interests, though, her laughter dimmed.

"What one of us did the others had to do too," Damian said. "When I became fascinated with medieval battles and the King Arthur legend, the three of us mowed lawns and did odd jobs until we had enough to buy everyone a reproduction shield and sword. My folks were tolerant and let me charge the leather pants, cape and chain mail from a catalog on their credit card. It took me six months of working for my mom to pay it off. She drives a hard bargain."

A shiver slid down her spine as Damian demonstrated his sword hold. His scar, those eyes, his easy grace with a blade…they were so familiar. They not only belonged to the man across from her but the man of her dreams as well. The man she'd fantasized about for years but whose face she'd only caught in glimpses.

"We always had a fair maiden to save, too," Damian said. "Imaginary, naturally, but we couldn't play hero without one. The other guys chose Wonder Woman but me, I rescued someone else."

His voice softened. "I used to see her in my dreams. Honey blonde hair, eyes blue like a darkening sky…I hated waking up."

Jessi's chest tightened and her throat closed. He could be describing her. And maybe he was. She'd always more of a literature than a science person so she didn't know much about the laws of time and space, or about other dimensions. Had they lived parallel lives, he on one plane and she on another, until a magical spell dissolved the barrier between them?

"We probably need to get home." She jumped up, nearly knocking over the cute wire-backed chair. "Mom's going to wonder what happened to us."

She pretended not to see the slight frown that crossed Damian's face. Yeah, she'd watched all those movies like "Weird Science" as a kid, but she didn't believe in that stuff.

She was pretty sure she didn't, anyway.

***

Molly hummed as she worked in the kitchen. She felt as if this old house had come back to life with Jessi and her friend here. Her step held a spring as she remembered how excited he'd been to see her little girl at the airport and how cute Jessi had been, holding back her emotions because Molly was watching.

They'd have beautiful children. He was tall enough to add a little height to the family, too. She'd never minded being only a few inches over five feet, but she knew Jessi had always wanted to be taller. Maybe her daughter would be.

Molly sighed, smiled and folded her hands across her heart. Grandchildren.

She'd started to believe she'd never have any. When her friends began bragging about theirs, it was all she could do to listen. For heaven's sake, she didn't even have a granddog. She'd tried to get Jessi to take a cute puppy from the shelter. That went over like a lead balloon. Apparently African violets were enough company in the city.

Maybe watching Becky get married would set things in motion. Jessi had always been a planner, making sure every detail was nailed down before she'd do anything. Time was flying; this engagement better be short. She refused to have to be helped down the aisle because she was too old to walk under her own steam.

Switching to a different tune, she kept on

humming as she started the meatloaf, checked the cheesecake in the oven and imagined holding her grandchild for the first time.

"Hi, Mom."

"Oh!" Startled, Molly almost knocked the mixing bowl off the counter. She glanced at the clock. It was only noon. That had been a short introduction to Durkin.

"Did you kids get hot?" she asked, blushing when she belatedly realized what she'd caught them doing on the porch. For heaven's sake, she'd have to watch herself while they were here.

"We cooled off with ice cream." Jessi sat cross-legged on one of the solid wooden chairs with an ease Molly envied.

"I love that little place." Molly patted the meatloaf into shape and placed it in a baking pan, continuing to talk as she washed her hands. "Do you remember Steven Carrothers? His sister's the one who opened it after she got a divorce and came back home."

The look that crossed Jessi's face told Molly she'd spoken without thinking again. Of course her girl remembered Steven. She'd doodled his name all over her notebooks and whispered about him to her girlfriends. No one forgot their first crush, not even if they wound up with someone so much better.

Deciding it might be better to listen than to talk, she asked Damian what he thought of her town. She was pleased when he praised it. She wasn't quite sure what the man did for a living, but she was certain he could do it here as well as anywhere else in the world. And Jessi could keep on working, too, with a grandma around to babysit.

Chapter Four

"Why don't you show your boyfriend the lake? You used to spend all your time up there as a teenager."

Jessi sat stone still. The reason she spent so much time there was because the back side of Crimson Lake was where kids went to smoke pot, drink beer and/or dance to music their parents didn't appreciate. She's been too chicken for either pot or beer and too insecure to skinny dip like some of her bolder friends. But she had done her share of making out during the summer after her senior year, although she was certain her mother never had a clue.

"Yeah, why don't you show me the lake?" Damian's eyes danced as he echoed Molly's words.

"If you need swimming trunks, I'm sure I can rustle some up." Molly headed toward the second floor before Jessi could stop her.

"Do not encourage her." Jessi shook her finger in Damian's face. "Before long she'll have us buckled in the car and heading for the amusement park."

"That's okay. I like cotton candy."

"You're as bad as she is." Jessi rolled her eyes. Mr. Mysterious was supposed to be her ideal man, not a co-conspirator with her mother. He was supposed to make her pulse race and her nerves vibrate, not spur her mom along memory lane.

Looking herself in the mirror ten minutes later, she wondered how many new ways to humiliate her mother could find. The pink checked bikini she'd worn in college had been perfect then. But she wasn't twenty-one anymore and she would have been much happier in a sleek black tankini. The only other choice her mother had offered, however, was her own blue skirted suit and Jessi wasn't quite ready for the matronly look yet.

Stepping out of her room, she waited in the hall for Damian who was changing behind his own closed door. She slapped her hands across her mouth to stifle laughter when he stepped out and struck a pose.

"Oh…my…" She managed between fits of giggles. Her Adonis, this magnificent specimen of outrageous manhood, had a pair of tropical print swim shorts. Huge red hibiscus warred with giant yellow fish for attention; the look was perfected by the high waist of the shorts.

"You're not seriously going out in public like that," she said when she could finally speak.

"Would you prefer that I wear a business suit? Or my boxers?"

The giggles started again as Jessi pictured Damian wading into the lake waters in a pair of those incredibly expensive silk boxers she'd seen him putting away. Oh dear heavens, she had to gain control of herself. She was so not like this.

A shout from her mother that she'd packed them snacks forced Jessi to take several deep breaths and head down the stairs, Damian on her heels. She slapped back playfully at him when he said in a stage whisper, "Now there's the best view in town."

The heat hit her as soon as they walked out the door and she was glad she had decided on an oversized cotton tee as a cover-up. The little breeze there was blew against her skin but held the warmth of the day. She offered the keys to her mother's car to Damian who shook his head and suggested she drive since she knew the town. She took the long way to the lake, taking the narrow back road that led to the non-guarded beach area.

"So this is the scene of the crime, huh?" Damian

asked as she parked on a patch of sun-dappled grass near the lake's edge.

"Scene of many crimes," she corrected. "Not mine necessarily but lots of others. Like Becky and Tim. I thought she was so cool, drinking beer and staying out after midnight."

"And what was your downfall?"

"Sexy men." Jessi cocked her hip and gave him her best come-hither look. "Even ones in ugly trunks."

"You've gone too far now, woman." One quick reach and she was tight against his body, looking up into his laughing face, trapped by his arms. "If we weren't in a public place…"

An empty public place where no one can see.

Did she whisper those words to him or did he read her thoughts? Did it matter as he acted on her impulse, dropping kisses along her neck, his hands cupping her bikinied bottom?

His lips were magic. Her body tightened, sizzling more from the heat within than the sun shining down on them. A moan escaped as his fingers slid under the fabric of the swim suit bottom to tease and explore. She quivered under his touch, gasped as his fingers slid

Page 75

inside her, shuddered as he brought her to the edge. The sound of tires of gravel penetrated her consciousness as Damian swept her up and carried her into the concealing waters of the lake.

She began to float when he released her, opening her eyes at the splash as Damian dove underwater and emerged a few yards away.

"Come get me!" he called, swimming around her in large loops.

Jessi dropped underwater and popped back up, tossing her head back to let the water run from her hair down her back. The fire raging through her calmed but her disappointment was much slower to dissipate. Time was rushing by. She shoved back the realization of how few days were left before she was scheduled to step onto a plane and return to Chicago and her real life and cut through the water toward Damian.

Her fingers almost touched him before he was gone again. Determination propelled her as she fell into the familiar routine of play. In and out of the water she went, following Damian's lead until she finally caught him. Or rather, he let her catch up by treading water until she dropped her arms around his neck and whispered "Gotcha."

"Took you long enough." Amusement colored his voice.

"Just giving you a head start." Jessi pushed away and swam back toward the sand. She glanced toward the parking area. They were alone again.

"You can't escape that easily." Damian took advantage of her distraction to grab her and turn her toward him. Treading water, holding her against him, he captured her lips again. She welcomed the kiss, acutely aware as his teeth gently took her lower lip, the feel of his hands moving down her back to cup her bottom, the intensity of her reaction to his very presence. The water lapped against them as she wound her arms around his neck again. The thin fabric of the bikini didn't stifle the sensation of her hardened nipples against his taut chest, the pressure of his erection against her.

Jessi opened her mouth willingly to his tongue. She settled against him, legs around his waist. A moan escaped when he thrust against her gently, teasing her, a keen reminder of how long it had been since she'd had sex.

"We stop now or we go all the way." His words

came in a tortured whisper. A tingle of triumph ran through her; he wanted her every bit as badly.

"We..."

Before she could breathe out "all the way", horns honked and graveled sprayed.

"Damn. Company's coming."

Damian captured her mouth once more in a quick kiss of promise. Jessi pushed away and dove underwater, heading for the line of buoys marking the end of the swimming area. She came up and began swimming hard, burning off the almost-there of their foreplay. When she reached the marker, she turned and swam toward shore with her eyes closed. She forced herself to concentrate on the strokes of her arms, turning her head to catch a breath, anything but the man she was dying to sleep with.

Damian was already on the beach and drying off when she got to the shoreline. He handed her a towel without speaking. Jessi scrubbed it across her dripping head before wiping her legs, arms and torso. She wrapped it around her body as another carload of teenagers pulled up and began claiming their space on the beach.

"Ready to go?" she asked.

The peace of the afternoon was about to morph into a cacophony of shouts and taunts. She knew that from her own growing up years. This was still the place where kids came to get away from their folks without getting in trouble.

"There's a picnic table over there." Damian pointed to a wooden table with built-on benches under a buckeye tree.

"And there's a couple of kids with a cooler." She tipped her head toward a pick-up that had just parked. She was sure the cooler with filled with soft drinks and beer as well as hot dogs. This group was settling in for an afternoon swim followed by an evening of being kids. "Let's go over to the shelter houses."

Jessi pulled her tee over her bikini. Damian threw on a button-down shirt that he left open and, like Jessi, spread his towel over the car seat to keep the dampness of their suits from soaking in.

One of the shelter houses was in use at the next pull-in, but the single tables were unused. Jessi grabbed the bag of snacks and drinks and led the way to one in a shady spot. She wasn't accustomed to the midday summer sun anymore.

"This was nice of your mom," he said. "She's pretty cool."

"That's because you don't know her well," Jessi countered. "Trust me, put one toe in the hallway between our rooms after we're supposed to be in bed and you'll see the evil side of Molly Abigail Flint."

Damian raised an eyebrow. "Then I suppose I'll have to have my way with you somewhere other than a bed. I'm open to suggestions, especially since the nights are so warm."

Jessi felt the dratted flush warm her cheeks. Now only was he the man of her fantasies, she suspected he knew her fantasies, like under a full moon in a grassy field pretending to be a princess cavorting with a stable hand. Or an old West lady of the night entertaining a sexy cowboy who had just come back from a cattle drive.

Not that she was about to confirm that.

"I say we have our way with the food," she said. "I'm starved."

She really was. Between ice cream for breakfast, skipping lunch and her hard swim, she had the appetite of a longshoreman. She began unpacking the plastic containers of food that her mother had called snacks but was really a meal. Ignoring the manners she taught, Jessi grabbed a fried chicken leg and bit into it without waiting for Damian.

She'd almost forgotten what a great cook her mother was. Even cold, the chicken was crisp and delicious. With those first bites eaten, she picked up a foam plate and loaded it with a second chicken leg, mustard potato salad and a fruit salad her mother always called ambrosia.

Being with Damian meant she could be herself. After all, he wouldn't be around for the long run. She figured conjured beings had an expiration date like milk. A few more days until the reunion and wedding were over, and he'd be gone as mysteriously as he appeared. So why not enjoy food instead of picking at it like a delicate flower to impress him?

"I love the way you eat."

"Excuse me?" Jessi stopped, her fork full of potato salad halfway to her mouth.

"With gusto. Enjoying both the flavor and the experience."

So chowing down like a little piggy turned him on. She could live with that especially since she knew the reunion potluck would include all the foods she couldn't get back home.

****

"Now what?" Damian stowed the picnic basket back in the trunk and turned to Jessi.

"You've toured the town. About the most exciting thing to do is going to the grocery's bakery and watch them frost the cookies."

He laughed, the sound rich and enticing. Of course, everything about this man was proving to be enticing.

"How about that historical museum I saw?"

"The old Belmont house? Sure. I hate to admit this, but I've never been there either."

"So we embark on a new adventure." Damian opened the passenger door for her before rounding the car to slip behind the wheel. Following her instructions, he drove the short distance back to the center of town and parked in front of the ornate brick Victorian house. An open sign hung crookedly on the front door.

Jessi had always loved this house, even during

its seedier days. She'd been in middle school when a historical society formed to save the building; she made a mental note to send a donation after she got back home. The place was striking now. Bright blooms filled rounded gardens beside the house and the iron railing that lined the wraparound porch looked like it had just received a new coat of black paint.

A white-haired lady with a cheery smiled chirped a hello when they stepped inside. Jessi wasn't surprised when, after signing the guest book, she was stopped by the volunteer.

"Oh, you're Molly's girl," she said. "I knew you looked familiar when you walked in but I couldn't quite place you. Is this your beau?"

"Uh-huh." Jessi smiled at the thought of anyone applying that old-fashioned term to Damian.

"Well, you kids can find your way through. I'll be right down here if you have any questions."

Jessi was surprised how many things she didn't know about Durkin, considering that she'd spent the majority of her life here. She was also impressed with Damian's interest in the museum exhibits, especially the ones detailing the town's involvement with the early

Page 83

auto industry.

The third floor held a gallery of old photographs. Jessi wandered from photo to photo, trying to place buildings that had long since been demolished and houses that still existed but had been dramatically changed.

"Hey, Jess." Damian's voice called to her. "Is this part of your family?"

She joined him at a portrait of a stern-faced man with a long beard and intense eyes. She looked at the card beside it.

Jeremiah Flint, circuit-riding preacher and early settler. He was known for his fire-and-brimstone sermons, being a fine furniture craftsman and outliving four wives who gave him a total of fourteen children.

"He sounds like a very busy man," Damian said. Jessi noticed his lips trembling a bit, like he was stifling a laugh.

"Especially when he got home from all that preaching," she said. "Do you think he got started making furniture by building beds? I bet he wore out a few."

Damian's chuckle set her off. She held her hand

against her mouth, trapping her laughter from echoing throughout the museum. She definitely did not want to explain to the pleasant docent why she was cackling her head off.

Avoiding Damian's eyes, she walked toward a group of school photos from before the Durkin School was consolidated into the county system. She was surprised to find both her mother's and her father's graduation pictures among them. She reached out and touched her dad's face. Her mother had changed over the years, but she would have recognized his dancing eyes and oval face anywhere. Tears prickled against her eyelids. She missed him so much. He'd been her most loyal supporter and greatest cheerleader. His support had given her the courage to step out on her own and begin her business. Yet he'd died before she had a chance to show him her success.

"You okay?"

She nodded and leaned against Damian, who'd come to stand behind her. "Yeah. Just looking at my folks in those pictures."

He wrapped his arms around her waist but didn't speak. She appreciated the quiet moment, this chance for her to deal in her own way with this sudden emotion. It was if he'd known she needed to come here.

"Any questions?" The docent stepped into the room, brochures in her hands. "I'd like to give you each one of these. We'll be having our Founder's Day celebration come fall; all the details are in there."

The interruption was what Jessi needed. She had come to Durkin for a joyful reason, and here she was going all maudlin.

Damian took the brochures with a smile of thanks and they headed back down the wooden steps to the second floor. Jessi viewed the collection of household objects that had been the big thing in their time with a sense of gratitude that she's never had to use them. She enjoyed looking at the wringer washer and heavy irons but was grateful for permanent press and a washer that worked with the press of a button.

"More photos." Damian led her into an alcove by the exit.

"More old photos," Jessi corrected as they walked in. They wandered from picture to picture making comments on the antique fashions and the stern expressions on nearly every face. Jessi bumped into

Damian's back as he stopped short at one particular on the far wall.

"She's smiling." His voice was tender. Jessi stepped around him to take a look.

"That looks like me." A strange sensation enveloped her.

"Don't remember posing for it, huh?" Damian slipped an arm around her waist.

Jessi glanced at the plaque next to the framed image that read "Unknown woman, circa 1850." A shiver ran through her; Damian's arms tightened around her.

"Ready to go?" he whispered. She nodded and took quick steps toward the door.

The afternoon light was dimming by the time they left the museum and drove back to the house. Molly greeted them with questions about their time out and an offer of iced tea which they drank on the porch. By the time they'd both showered and dressed, dinner was on the table.

"Another fantastic meal." Damian patted his flat midriff. "Keep this up and you're going to have to roll me out of here."

Molly waved a hand of dismissal at him, although her face was wreathed in a smile. Once again, Jessi was impressed by the way her mother and the supposed love of her life had connected. If only this was real…

*****

Those two were meant for each other. Molly had known it from the moment she'd seen them together. The light in Damian's eyes when he saw her, the trembling way in which her little girl had stepped into his arms…true love couldn't be hidden.

The one thing that bothered her was why Jessi hadn't told her about him. She'd always confided the important things in her life, even those early crushes when she first discovered boys. Her calls were full of information about her business and where she'd been and the various events she went to from time to time. Yet she'd never said a word about this man.

A terrible thought crossed her mind. Maybe he'd been married when she met him.

She stopped with her hands in the soapy dishwater. Maybe he was still married.

The implications of her Jessi being in love with a

wedded man preoccupied Molly as she went through the mechanical details of washing the dishes and putting them away. Surely her daughter hadn't known he was married when they met. Jessi's morals were far too high for that.

Perhaps his wife was one of those shrews who trapped him into a loveless marriage and wouldn't let him go. But that might mean he had children. And one thing Molly was against was the breakup of the family.

She poured herself a cup of coffee and sat down at the kitchen table. Jessi and Damian were watching the news on TV in the other room, so she had a little time to herself. She needed it, too. No way could she confide in her friends or family members. She was not about to ruin his reputation and their relationship with nothing more than a gut feeling to go on.

Destinee. She realized that if anyone knew the details, it had to be Jessi's secretary. And she also knew that Destinee would be willing share that knowledge. Tomorrow, while Jessi was off getting fitted for her bridesmaid's dress, she'd make the call and find the truth. She gave a sign of satisfaction and went to join the others. The answer was only a few hours away.

Chapter Five

Jessi had the distinct feeling her mother had something on her mind. But before she could ask – or Mom could offer – the doorbell rang. She jumped to see who it was opened the door with delight to her best high school friend, Heather.

"Oh my gosh, you look wonderful!" She offered a big hug of welcome.

"I look pregnant. Again." Heather handed over a tin with a snowman motif. "My mother sent these. You still like molasses cookies, right?"

"Of course." She pulled the top off the tin and took an appreciative sniff. "Come in and sit down."

She'd forgotten about Damian. Her memory loss was short-lived when Heather stopped and said in a stage whisper, "Excuse me, have you been hiding something?"

"I'm her eye candy." Damian stood and offered his hand. "That's what she said when she invited me to come to Becky's wedding. That and she needs someone to carry her purse while she serves as maid of honor."

"He is so lying." Jessi played it off with a laugh. "This is Damian St. Clair, my…"

When she paused to find the right word, her mother finished with "fiancé. Yes, Jessi has finally decided to tie the knot."

Jessi was subjected to another hug and a million questions including how soon the wedding would take place.

"We haven't even talked about dates." That, at least, wasn't a lie. "Right now, I'm only worrying about everything going on this week."

"Oh my gosh, can you believe Becky's putting a wedding together so fast? I mean it's no surprise they want to get married before Tim leaves, but she's going to have a ceremony that rivals the Queen of England's."

The two old friends sat down on the couch and starting catching up on things. Jessi uttered a mindless okay when Damian said he was going upstairs to read and nodded when her mother announced that she was going for her nightly walk. She should have realized that once she and Heather were alone, she'd get the grilling of a lifetime.

"So where did you find him?" Heather adjusted

her position, plopping her feet on the coffee table as she'd always done. "And why have you not loaded down your social sites with pictures of the two of you? He is beyond gorgeous and you know it."

"We don't spend that much time together," Jessi said in what might be the understatement of the century. "I have my business travels, he has his. You know how it goes."

"No. No, I do not. My life is one big cycle of cooking, laundry and either putting kids to bed or getting them up. This will be my fourth, you know. I've pretty much forgotten what having a life is like."

"Oh, come on, you know you're perfectly happy with Ryan and the kids. They must provide all sorts of entertainment."

"True, but don't change the subject. We're talking about you and the sexiest man alive, remember? Details, I want details."

Which was the one thing Jessi didn't have. She should have been working on a story long before she stepped off the plane. Except, of course, she hadn't believed a magic man would be waiting for her with her mother. Nor had she remembered that in a small town, everyone felt obliged to ask questions, especially old friends. She fished in her memory trying to remember what Damian had told her mother. Coffee shop…food…

"Our lunch orders got switched at this little place down from my office." She forced warmth into her voice, like she so loved to tell the story. "From then on it seemed like we ran into each all the time and finally he asked me to dinner. I said yes and that was that."

"Perfect." Heather settled back against the couch. "Remember those romance novels we traded around in high school? You two could be living in one."

Well, some sort of fiction, like a fairy tale.

"You coming to all the reunion stuff?" The question was deliberate attempt to change the focus of the conversation. It worked.

"Between moms, we've arranged a schedule." Heather rolled her eyes. "It was so much easier before Noah started playing ball and Lindsey began ballet lessons. One of the mothers will stay at our place with the baby while the other one gets where they need to go. I will owe some fantastic Christmas presents this year, believe me."

Listening to Heather rattle on, Jessi couldn't

believe there were times she was jealous of her married with children friends. Something in Heather's tone made her wonder if it didn't work the other way at times. Her own life of travel and an independent business sounded good until she found herself facing delayed flights, delinquent payments and the constant need to sell her services to enough people to keep the doors open and cash flowing steady.

She'd always pictured herself with a husband and couple of kids but now she wondered if she could actually manage it. After this week was over and she returned to her manless, hectic life back in Chicago, being honorary auntie to Becky's future children might be enough to satisfy that maternal need.

"Okay, the biggest question of all." Heather leaned forward, grabbed Jessi's shoulders and looked right at her. "Have you seen your dress yet?"

"Oh, no." Jessi's eyes widened. "The fitting is tomorrow. If it's hideous beyond compare tell me now so I don't faint in shock at the dress shop."

Heather dropped back. "I was hoping you could tell me. I saw the different pictures she'd marked in the shop's catalog and thought she may have come to her senses."

"A general theme?" Jessi probed.

"Add a parasol and a mint julep to any of them and you'll be right in style. As long as it's the 1800s and you're hanging with Scarlett O'Hara."

Visions of multi-layered dresses with flounces everywhere danced through Jessi's mind. She'd never been happy with her hips but she managed to camouflage them through careful dressing. A big southern belle dress would make her look like a flat-footed hippo when she preceded Becky down the aisle.

She so hoped the dress would be blue or green or anything but Becky's favorite two colors, purple or orange. Or purple and orange. She wouldn't be all surprised if her cousin had somehow secured one in just that combination.

"Wanna come with us tomorrow?" she asked. Heather had been on the high school debate team and might be able to talk Becky into something a little less circus-ish.

"Can't. Noah has a dentist's appointment. Take your mother with you."

"Sure." Jessi rolled her eyes. "She still thinks

I'm ten years old and ought to wear white Mary Janes and little sundresses. She'd side with Becky in a heartbeat."

"Then drag along the gorgeous being upstairs. I bet he has no trouble talking women into anything."

As if he'd been summoned, Damian walked into the living room carrying the pitcher of iced tea and offered refills. Both women accepted; Heather suggested he sit down and join them. Jessi knew her friend was going to start fishing but she had no problem with that. Heather's inquisition should reveal things she ought to know but her supposed soul mate. Instead the conversation became a recitation of the most embarrassing moments in Jessi's life, happily supplied by Heather.

"So there she was, trapped by that big hoop skirt trying to exit the stage in a graceful manner," her supposed friend recalled about the one and only time Jessi had participated in a beauty pageant. "I was so proud of her, though. Her smile didn't falter until she stepped on the edge of the hoop, tipped it up to her chin and fell back on her butt. She may not have won, but Jessi was the most memorable participant."

Damian's laughter filled the room, so rich and masculine that Jessi almost forgave him for cracking up. Almost. She shot Heather a "do it again and you'll die" look, stood up and said in a voice so like her mother's that it scared her, "Why don't we all have some ice cream?"

"Sounds good," Damian said at the same time that Heather said, "I can't. Ryan will never get the kids to bed if I'm not there to help."

The house seemed strangely silent once they were alone. The silence was companionable, as if they knew each other well enough not to have to fill the spaces with noise or conversation. Like it would be if this whole thing with Damian was real.

Dammit, it was for the next few days.

She took Damian's hand and pulled him from the couch. The clock would strike midnight again and she'd be a modern-day Cinderella once more. Except in her particular fairy tale, the prince wouldn't be showing up with a glass slipper and a proposal. She didn't know how all these fantastical things worked, but she was pretty sure you couldn't petition for an extension. Once he was gone, that was that. They'd already wasted enough time.

"Yoo-hoo, kids, I'm back." The words were immediately followed by the slamming of the back screen door, a little harder than necessary. Apparently her mother wanted to make sure she wasn't interrupting anything.

Still holding Damian's hand, Jessi went into the kitchen where her mother was pouring herself a glass of sweet tea. After the obligatory questions about how her walk had been and the catching up on the small town news her mother had gathered, Molly crossed her arms across her chest, tipped her head and said, "You know I'm capable of entertaining myself. Honey, why don't you and Damian go out for a while?"

"Uh, because we're in Durkin?"

Molly laughed. "That never stopped you when you were younger."

"Good point." Jessi tossed Damian the keys to his rental. "We'll be back pretty soon."

"Take your time." Molly gave Damian a pointed stare. "I believe we've already established the ground rules."

He smiled and sketched a salute. "Gentlemanly

behavior at all times and no slipping into her room after we retire. I remember every word."

"Maybe we'll go bowling," Jessi said. "The Imperial Lanes is still around, I hope?"

Her mother's cheeks pinkened but her voice sounded normal as she said, "Yes, dear. I'm sure Damian will enjoy the place. Your father did."

Her cheeks were a bright red by the last word. Jessi was dying to know why but Molly's act of turning to the dishwasher as if unloading it was of dire importance was a definite barrier. It wasn't until she was inside the car with Damian that she realized why her mother blushed.

Dad had bowled in a Saturday night league for years. He'd always kissed Molly on the cheek and whispered something to her as he left but Jessi had only caught the words once. She'd been too young and naïve to understand his ribald remark then but now she knew the meaning. No wonder her mom had been embarrassed; what she'd overheard so long ago was "I'm gonna go warm up my balls, honey."

She shook her head and said "It's nothing" when Damian asked why she was smiling. Without seeing her parents together, he wouldn't understand how much they'd loved each other and kept loving each other until Dad's death.

They rode with the windows down and a Detroit radio station playing on their way to Monroe, the get-away town for folks from Durkin. The bowling alley was the same building but it had been given a facelift since she'd been there last. How long had it been? Five years? Ten?

Instead of walking up to rent shoes and pay for a few games, Jessi led Damian into the lounge area. Separated by a glass wall from the lanes, it was a throwback to the 1960s, right down to the jukebox providing a neon shimmer in a corner. A small stage at the front held microphones and instrument stands; the tradition of local bands playing on the weekends hadn't changed either.

The one thing different was the menu. Instead of the old burger and fries selections, this one offered barbecue sliders, chicken wings and even healthy choices like a spinach salad. Jessi searched for the most retro snack available and finally decided on chili cheese fries. She'd never indulge in them at home, let alone on a date, but she was on vacation. And this wasn't a date. This was…she still didn't know.

Chapter Six

Molly stared at the number jotted on the small piece of paper. Should she or shouldn't she?

She took a deep breath, picked up the phone and dialed. Any time, day or night. That was exactly what Destinee had said in giving her cell number. And nine o'clock wasn't all that late, especially for a young person like Jessi's secretary. She counted the rings; if Destinee didn't answer by the fourth one, she would hang up.

A chirpy "Hello!" came across the line just after ring three. Molly felt a momentary panic; if Jessi found out…

"I hope I'm not interrupting anything," she said, ready to hang up if she had.

"Only the last bite of butter brickle ice cream and a rerun of 'Seinfeld'," Destinee replied. "I much prefer real people. So how are things going there?"

"Quite well so far." Molly searched for the right way to frame her question. "But my daughter is less than forthcoming. She seems happy, yet it feels like she's keeping a secret from me. Is there more between them than she's letting on?"

A wave of relief rolled through her. There. She'd said it out loud. Her common sense, down to earth Jessi might be hiding a huge secret. Like that she was cohabitating with her handsome man with no intention of marriage.

"They made a really fast connection," Destinee replied after a slight hesitation.

"I'll say! I had no idea she was seeing someone let alone talking about marriage."

"Well, you know how private Jessi can be. I didn't even learn about it until, like, just a little while ago."

"Oh." Destinee's confession made Molly feel a little bit better. Her daughter hadn't been keeping news of Damian from just her; she'd hidden her relationship from everyone.

"They're getting along, right?"

Molly laughed. "You could light a fire with the sparks between them sometimes. I sent them off to spend a little time alone before tomorrow's dress fitting."

"Ooh, send me a picture. I so need to see what

Jessi will be wearing."

"I promise. Trust me, Becky's selected something memorable."

"You may want to check out her closet," Destinee suggested. "I tried to talk her into buying something sexy for the reunion dinner but I bet she brought a suit."

"If she did, I'm hiding it. All eyes will be on Jessi when she walks in with Damian so she needs to look attractive."

"Hot," Destinee corrected. "Any chance you can go along tomorrow and make her buy a new dress?"

That, Molly knew, would be a challenge. Even if she bought the perfect dress for Jessi, she couldn't make her stubborn daughter wear it. But she knew someone who could.

"While she's with Becky, I'll take Damian into town," she decided. "He probably knows her taste as well as I do by now, don't you think? And if he gives it to her, she'll be excited to wear it."

"Yeah, I'd go with that." Destinee's voice sounded more thoughtful had ever heard, more thoughtful. "You may want to remind her that her vacation will be over soon and she needs to make the most of her days in Durkin."

That change in Destinee's voice kept Molly from pressing for details as she'd planned. Could there be a problem between those two that Jessi was hiding?

"I'll be sure to do that. Now I'd better let you get back to your show."

With mutual goodbyes, the conversation was over. Molly poured herself a glass of iced tea and went out into the warm evening air. There was just enough breeze to make sitting on the porch comfortable and enough neighbors out for an evening stroll to keep her mind off the kids. She would not be one of those interfering mothers who ended up bashed on their child's blog. Jessi was a full-grown woman whose life was her own.

Molly sighed and longed for just a moment for those days when Jessi hadn't made a single decision without asking her opinion, whether it was about boys or hairstyles.

****

"We're really bowling?"

"Afraid I'll beat you too badly?"

"Like that could happen. My father, who carried a 250 average, taught me everything I know."

"So go find a ball and let's do this thing."

Jessi regretted her brave words with her first throw which curved off the wood and into the gutter. She wasn't surprised when Damian got a strike his first time up.

She attempted to ignore his smile as she picked up her own blue ball and stepped up to the line. Taking a deep breath, she ran through her remembered advice from her father. Squaring her shoulders, she kept her elbows at her sides, moved slowly forward and released the ball at the end of her swing. She was delighted when eight pins fell; the two still standing were tucked together in the corner.

"Thought you had me, didn't you?" She flashed a grin toward Damian as she waited for the ball to return.

"Still do."

"Pretty cocky, aren't you?"

Damian stepped behind her as she picked up the ball. Speaking softly into her ear, he said, "Sure enough to make a bet."

Jessi turned and met his dancing eyes. "Name it."

"I win, you cross the hall."

Her eyes still locked on his, she answered, "I win, we go back to the lake."

"Deal." His lips brushed hers and his fingers traced an X across the left side of her chest. "Cross your heart."

Jessi felt the tingle all the way to her toes. Sticking her fingers in the ball and stepping up to the line was a whole lot harder this time. What happened when they left here was inevitable. Only the location was up for grabs.

She closed her eyes, tried to clear the images of being naked with Damian and forced herself to concentrate on the moment. Opening her eyes, she once again took a deep breath, timed her steps and let the ball roll. The slam of the pins falling brought a shout of triumph welling from her.

"Very nice." Damian brushed against her hip as he crossed to the ball return. The touch made her shiver as she dropped into a seat to see what happened next. She wasn't too surprised when a perfectly-placed ball slammed ten pins down again. She should expect nothing less of a magical creation, after all.

The game ended as she expected with Damian raising his arms in victory. She bowed in surrender, laughing with him as they changed shoes and headed out into the night.

"That was fun." Damian unlocked the passenger door and held it open for her.

"It's been a long time since I've let go like that," she said, sliding onto the seat. "Still, I think it's best that we don't tell my mother I stomped my foot and called you a butthead when you got that last strike."

"We'll keep it our secret." Jessi heard him chuckle as he closed the door and went around to his own side. She expected him to buckle up and fire up the engine but instead he turned toward her and cupped his chin with his hand.

"You don't have to keep our bet," he said. "After all, I promised Molly we'd behave in her house."

Jessi felt a rush of disappointment. Her anticipation had built all evening as they'd touched and flirted, well aware that the challenge would go to Damian. Now that she knew he wasn't going to disappear in a puff of smoke or melt away, she didn't want to waste a moment left to them.

"But I think I remember the way to the beach." He dropped a kiss on her lips before pulling away to start the car and pull out onto the highway. The miles sped away as he ran over speed limit and found the park entrance without error.

"That way." Jessi pointed to a side road shortly before the turnoff for the swimming area. "And take it slow."

A few hundred yards later, she directed him to pull off in a narrow parking area. They walked hand in hand down a path lit only by moonlight, Damian carrying the blanket he'd brought from the back seat of the car. Jessi led him into a small clearing along the edge of the water and waited while he spread the blanket on the ground.

"You know I was a good girl in high school, right?" She slipped her hands around the hard muscles of his upper arms.

Damian nodded.

"Even good girls have fantasies." She moved to within inches of him, her fingers slipping up to clasp at the back of his neck.

"Oh, do they?" Damian's arms wrapped around her waist.

"Mine was to do naughty things up here at the make out place of my youth."

"You're lucky. I know all about naughty."

"I remember."

Damian offered a lifted eyebrow and a wicked grin before his lips met hers. Jessi curled into him as anticipation rolled through her. The teasing touches and the embraces they'd shared combined with the promise of making love with Prince Charming melted her inhibitions. She rose to her toes and pressed against him, Damian's scent blending with the lake breeze, his heart beating faintly against her own.

Something between a sigh and a moan escaped from her as Damian loosened his hold and clasped the hem of her tee to slide it over her head. She stood still as his fingers moved down to unbutton the waist of her shorts and slide down the zipper. Tingles ran through her as he pushed the fabric down for her to step out of them. Clad only in her lace bra and panties, she dropped onto the blanket to watch as he began to undress.

He was every bit as magnificent as she'd imagined, from his wide shoulders to the erection jutting toward her. She thanked whatever force had created him as he lay down beside her and stroked her hair. The lapping of the water against the rocky shore and the faint noise of teenagers partying at the beach were the only sounds besides their own breathing.

Jessi lost herself in the tenderness of his lips, the stroking of his hands along her body, the sensations she'd suppressed without realizing it. She barely knew when he undid the clasp of her bra to free her breasts, only arched when his teeth teased first one taut nipple then the other. His fingers slid down her soft curves to slip beneath her panties and coax them off.

Nothing existed except this moment and this man as she gave herself up to the need pulsing through her. Fiery desire drove her as his mouth moved from her breasts down her stomach and then on to her tender womanhood, his tongue languid as she shuddered and gave in to the need to climax. Before she'd fully recovered, Damian filled her trembling body, strong strokes bringing her once again to the point of no return and beyond.

Page 111

His embrace was gentle as she came back to reality. She'd never experienced lovemaking like this. And, she feared, would never again once he left her. Tears filled her eyes at the thought of living without him.

"What's wrong?" Damian wiped the tears from her cheek.

"Nothing. Everything." She forced a smile. "Being back home, being with you, Becky getting married…it's all hit at once."

"I was afraid I'd done something wrong."

Jessi's smile was real as she looked into those dark, marvelous eyes. "Oh, no, you did everything right. Way beyond right."

****

The sound of the partying had faded by the time they dressed, folded up the blanket and headed back to the car. Jessi glanced at the clock as soon as Damian turned the key. Nearly two in the morning. She couldn't remember the last time she'd been out this late. Her routine had become early to bed and early to rise; she was often asleep before the late night news came on.

"If your mom's waiting up, we're in trouble."

Jessi laughed. "If my mom's waiting up, I'm having a talk with her. She may see me as her little girl, but I'm all grown up."

"Oh, yes indeed." Damian ran his hand along her thigh and she felt a corresponding rush of pleasure.

They returned to a house that was dark except for one lamp lit in the living room. Jessi waited until Damian was upstairs to turn it off. Even having been away for years, she knew every nook and cranny of this house as well as every loose floorboard.

Damian had waited for her. She eagerly accepted his good night kiss before entering her room with great reluctance. Tonight she wanted to be with him, to curl against him as she fell asleep. She doubted that he'd protest too much if she sneaked into his bed but she wasn't about to tempt him to break his promise.

She wasn't at all surprised the next morning to awaken again to the aroma of coffee and sound of conversation downstairs. She glanced at the bedside clock. Nearly ten o'clock. It hadn't taken long for her to abandon her habits.

Jessi winced as she got out of bed and headed for the shower. Her shoulders and thighs ached. Apparently jogging used different muscles than bowling. Maybe she needed to find a new exercise regime.

She put on dark slacks and a white shirt that she topped with a beige linen jacket. Becky would be here soon to pick her up for the dreaded dress reveal. Maybe if her cousin saw her in her usual conservative clothes, she'd rethink fluff and poufs. When Becky bounced in a half later in red jeans, gold flip flops and a purple tank top, Jessi realized she was fighting a lost cause. Resigned to what was to come, she grabbed her purse to follow Becky out the door.

"Excuse me," her cousin said, "but aren't you forgetting something?"

After a blank moment, Jessi realized she was expected to kiss Damian goodbye. This relationship thing was still too new for her to remember what other couples did without thinking. She rolled her eyes, as if to let them know what a ditz she was, and headed for where Damian still sat at the table.

"I'll walk you out," he said, rising with an easy grace. With Jessi's hand in his, he followed Becky into the warm midday heat. While she went on to the car, he held Jessi back and kissed her thoroughly. She was still a bit dazed when she joined Becky for the ride to the bridal shop. By the time they reached the parking lot, she was back in control and going, "Oh?" and "Uh, huh," throughout Becky's monologue on the church decorations and her mother's attempt to run everything.

The shop had a number of customers when they walked in but Becky was greeted with an immediate, "You're here!" from a middle-aged woman whose fashion sense synched with hers. Jessi hung back while the two hugged and chattered at each other. She couldn't understand a word either of them said but they seemed to have no problem. She realized she'd been the subject of that conversation when they turned as one and smiled at her.

"You are going to love your dress," said the clerk, whose name tag identified her as Louise. She swept her arm toward a bank of louvered doors and told Jessi to pick one.

Five minutes later, despite a deep desire to hide under the changing room bench where no one could find her, Jessi stepped out into the private show area to a gasp by Becky and a clapping of Louise's hands.

"It's perfect!" Becky clasped a hand to her chest.

"It isn't even going to need alterations, is it?"

"Oh, heavens no." Louise yanked here and adjusted there. "Honey, it's as if this was made just for you. Go look at yourself in that three-way mirror."

The last thing Jessi wanted was to see three views of herself gussied up like a southern belle attempting to blend in at a Brazilian carnival. The bright yellow sateen fabric reminded her of her tap dance costume in second grade although with about eight layers of ruffle less than her maid of honor dress. The glossy emerald green band at the waist mirrored the wide shoulder straps and pleated trim along the hem of the calf-length gown.

Still she obediently walked over the mirror and positioned herself right in the center. The view tripled was no better; the only saving grace, if there was one, turned out to be the lack of a giant bow in the back. She forced a smile, propped a hand on her hip and waited for an opinion.

"Something's missing," Becky said with a frown.

"Hair up!" Louise declared before toddling behind the counter to come back with a super-size plastic box. She dug through the contents with an occasional stop for a consultation with Becky. Her exclamation of "Aha!" brought new dread for Jessi. The dread was fulfilled after the clerk produced what looked like a spray of yellow-tipped purple orchids on a hair clip, pulled up Jessi's hair and popped the flowers on top.

"What do you think?" she asked while Jessi tried not to let her shock and dismay show.

Arms folded, head tipped, Becky studied the effect. Time crawled until finally, she announced "I think it might be a little bit too much."

Jessi choked back the words dying to come out like "You think?" and "Trust me, no one will notice with this dress." Becky was only going to have one wedding – so Jessi hoped – and she deserved to have everything just as she wanted. Even if everyone with a cell phone was going to pop a shot and post it online so Jessi's humiliation could go viral.

Louise dug through the box again. Off came the funeral spray and Jessi found herself with a feather and ribbon confection instead. The final touch was the little mesh veil that hit Jessi just at mid-eye making her vision a little wonky. She zoned out when the discussion turned to whether the white mesh could be dyed green to match the trim on her gown. Did it matter really? She'd only have to wear this thing once and maybe for an hour or so. The second the ceremony ended she'd change into something more her style. Which would be anything other than this fashion disaster.

"Oh, the shoes!" Louise disappeared behind a curtain and returned with a blue shoebox in her hands. Jessi wasn't at all surprised that the contents were a pair of satin pumps dyed yellow with a clipped-on red flower. Naturally, they fit perfect. Becky had always been great at guessing her size.

Her cell phone rang as they were loading the dress and bags of accessories into the back seat of Becky's car. She answered with a breathless "Hello?" just before it went to voice mail. Her heart lifted at Damian's "Need rescuing yet?"

"The worst is over." She walked to her side of the car but waited until her cousin had gotten in to speak again. "The dress was different than I envisioned but equally scary. Becky is on the verge of overload because she forgot to buy favors for the guest tables and I just got conned into writing out the place cards for the reserved seats." She opened the door and slid inside. "How's your day been?"

"I know how to make chocolate-dipped strawberries now. Your mother and I made six dozen for the shower. And about a million meat balls to go into barbecue sauce."

Jessi smiled at the image of Damian wearing one of her mom's over the head aprons and rolling ground beef into balls while her mother lectured him on the importance of keeping them uniform in size. Of course, she was sure they were perfect given who he was. What he was.

"I guess it is good you two are bonding," she said.

"Yeah." Humor colored his voice. "Since she told me about your first time behind the wheel and what happened with your bake sale cake in junior high."

"Oh…my…" She couldn't get more than those two words out. She loved her mother but it would be nice if she could pull out some stories that make her look wonderful. Like getting on the debate team as a freshman and being chosen to represent the school at the state mock government session.

"I've got to go." Damian's goodbye was hurried. "Molly wants to show me how to make napkin swans."

He was gone before Jessi could say goodbye or see you later. She stared at the screen blinking "call ended" at her and wondered whether she should rush home or just let her life fall to ruins without her. Her indecision dissipated when Becky asked if she wanted to stop for something to eat.

"We can go to Gilbert's," she teased. Those four words were enough for Jessi to forget about the mess of a dress, her mom's big mouth and how she was going to make it the rest of the week. Every town had a place like Gilbert's, a restaurant that had been in business for generations and always seemed the same. Great food, fantastic service and the plus of not being in Durkin, which meant she had an outside chance to relax and regroup.

She noticed immediately that the place had new paint. It was, naturally, the same red and white that had been Gilbert's theme for years. The original Gilbert had long retired but in his honor every manager had worn a name tag that read Gil ever since.

The current Gil, who looked to me younger than Jessi herself, seated them in the corner booth of their choice. After she and Becky were able to drive, they'd sometimes come here, sit there and share the trials and tribulations of being a teenage girl. In fact, it was right there that Becky had confessed she was thinking of "doing it" with Tim.

"I always thought you and Tim would get married right after high school," she said after the waitress brought their drinks and took their order.

"So did he." Becky gave a quick smile. "And his mother. I think that was the biggest reason I refused. I like his mom but she can be pretty bossy. I wanted to wait until he knew himself a little better before I hogtied him with a wedding ring."

"And yourself?"

"Yeah." Becky played with the straw in her soft drink. "I was jealous of you. Did you ever suspect?"

"Jealous of me?" Jessi was flabbergasted. Becky had been the pretty one, the star in the school plays, always in the homecoming court. And since she'd been every bit as nice, she'd had tons of friends in and out of school.

"You got away from here." Becky met her eyes. "While I was getting my associate's degree at the community college, working at the bank and dating Tim, you were living in a city where no one told on you. You could do what you wanted, whenever you wanted, without having to answer to a soul."

Jessi sat back in her seat, taking it in. Going to the University of Michigan had been a huge shock. Sitting in lecture halls with a hundred other students, trying to forge friendships with people who didn't even know where Durkin was, fighting off homesickness…that was what she remembered most of her first year there. And her first year after college, with a great title with a Fortune 500 company but being nothing more than a glorified secretary, had made her question her decision to strike out on her own. It was only in the last few years, since she'd started her company and watched it grow, that she no longer wished she had Becky's secure, predictable life.

"But while you were snuggling at the movies with Tim or joining his family for holidays, I was freaking out over my work load and then my finances," she finally said. "This independence thing isn't all it's cracked up to be."

With the appearance of their food, the conversation was abandoned. Jessi took a bite of the fat grilled ham and cheese sandwich and sighed. This place was still as good as ever. And even though she shouldn't, she ate all her food, down to the last piece of coating that fell off her onion rings. Giving in to temptation, she ordered a piece of blackberry pie when Becky did, although she had hers boxed to take home.

Becky caught her up on the way home on the general gossip of Durkin. Although she knew she'd never remember who got caught with another woman behind the lodge hall or which wife the local grocer was up to, she was quite content to listen. This was another thing she missed in her new life, the details that wove a community together.

Chapter Seven

The kitchen held the rich aroma of having been used all day. Jessi took an appreciative sniff as she walked in and debated the chance of her getting caught if she took just one of those strawberries. Her inclination to be bad was stopped by the appearance of her mother.

"Where's Damian?" she asked.

Her mother gave a smug smile. "He'll be right along."

A tremor of suspicion flitted through Jessi. If her mother and her supposed boyfriend were in cahoots, it could only mean trouble. Mom was an incurable romantic, after all.

When her mother suggested she go upstairs and get pretty, Jessi did what she was told. She was getting used to doing this easy, no-argument thing she'd fallen into since she'd come home.

The sound of the back door slamming carried up to her bedroom. She waited a few minutes before going back downstairs just in case the big surprise needed a little arranging. She was surprised to find the house empty.

"Mom?" she called. "Damian?"

No answer. She walked into the living room and even in her mom's bedroom but the place was deserted. Heading back to the kitchen, she stopped and shrieked when Damian stepped from the hall right into her path.

"Hey, I didn't mean to scare you." He gave her a quick hug. "I figure you were worn out from spending the day with your cousin and could use a little pampering."

"A little pampering?" If he planned to take her to some luxury spa for a facial and full-body massage, he was going to be severely disappointed. The closest Durkin had to either of those were the wrinkle creams sold at the grocery and the vibrating recliners some of the old-timers still had in their living rooms.

"I've made dinner reservations at a place Molly recommended…"

"The Hare and Sparrow," her mother interjected.

"And afterwards I thought maybe we'd go bowling again since we enjoyed it so much last night."

Jessi choked a little looking at her mom's face. Her trusting, encouraging face. If she knew what bowling led to the night before, she wouldn't be near as enthusiastic.

After a second trip upstairs, this time to change into something more suitable for the upscale restaurant, Jessi was back in a car again, heading out of town one more time. She was relaxed this time, mostly because no unpleasant surprises awaited her at their destination.

They were given one of the banquettes which helped close them off from the other diners. Jessi let Damian order for her; so far he'd made perfect choices and she loved not having to decide another thing. The wine he chose was aged and sweet; the steaks brought to them were perfectly done. She hadn't been surprised to hear him order hers medium-well even though he asked for his to be well done.

They ended the meal with rich cheesecake and a dessert wine recommended by the wine steward. She felt pampered and precious as they left the restaurant, his arm wrapped around her waist. The evening had been divine. It was such a marvelous change from her usual routine of grabbed meals and food between flights.

"Time for bowling," he said as he helped her into the car. But he passed the drive for Imperial Lanes and instead turned into the parking lot of one of the pricier chain motels.

"I checked and there is no five-star hotel closer than Detroit," he said. "But this place has a honeymoon suite with a hot tub. I hope that will do instead."

The room turned out to be far better than Jessi had expected. Calling it a suite was a stretch, but the hot tub was separated from the rest of the room that contained a timed fireplace, plush couch and round table and two upholstered chairs. An iced bucket sat in the center of the table with a bottle of what she was pretty sure was champagne already chilling. She walked into the second room to find a thick carpet, a huge bed and a basket of chocolates on the bedside table with a note of welcome.

"Very nice." She turned to Damian.

"Thank you." He took her hand and let her back to the other room. Seating her on the couch, he turned on the fireplace, poured the champagne into flutes and turned off the lights. Setting the stemmed glasses on the low table in front of them, he removed his suit jacket and tie, kicked off his shoes and then bent to remove her shoes as well. Jessi tensed; this was a first for her.

"Relax." His voice was low, husky. "I want to make you happy. You be Cinderella and I'll be your Prince Charming."

His words brought an ache. He was so, so perfect; she intended to remember every detail of this night. When she was back in the ordinary world, when her evenings went back to the television and reports, she'd pull this memory out to remind herself she'd had a fairy tale romance once.

Damian's movements were slow and teasing as he alternated taking off his own clothing and removing hers. His touch was gentle, his kisses teasing rather than demanding. She offered no resistance when he scooped her up and carried her to bed. She opened her arms in invitation when he hesitated.

"Let me adore you." He whispered the words as he stretched out to face her. Jessi tensed when his hand stroked from shoulder to hip, relaxed when his mouth captured hers. She grasped the rails of the mahogany head board as her body arched against his fingers, his lips, his tongue. A desperate need for satisfaction raced through her but Damian continued the exquisite torment despite her gasping pleas. When she knew she could take no more, when her body screamed for release, he plunged into her. Her wordless cry echoed through the room when one last thrust brought them both over the brink into ecstasy.

She collapsed against him, her limbs languid. Damian's arms closed around her and pressed her against him as he whispered sweet words to her. A final tremor shook her as her body began to recover.

"Shower?" He said, an invitation offered in that single word.

"You go first without me." Her voice stayed steady.

"You sure?" He propped himself on one elbow and looked down at her.

"No, but I think it's safer." Jessi gave him her best smile. "We do have to get home sometime before dawn."

"Yes, I know." She heard the regret in his voice.

She held it together until she heard the water start. Turning her face to the pillow, she let herself cry. He was perfect, this night had been perfect and dammit, she was in love with him. All these years of playing keep away with Cupid, and he'd managed to nick her now.

Destinee couldn't have known how the spell worked when she'd had her witchy woman cast it. Maybe the wish granter herself hadn't known that Jessi would fall hard for the man of her dreams. Or maybe this was a fairy tale turned into temporary reality, an opportunity for her to experience the kind of love not meant for her during this lifetime.

She allowed herself to ponder whether those dreams were truly from her imagination or if they were memories from a different incarnation. Could they have been lovers centuries ago?

Of course not. She shoved the thought away. People lived, they died. All those stories of reincarnations and eternal soul mates were flights of fancy. She and Destinee had talked about what they considered the perfect man. Her choice was tall, dark and mysterious. It was just a huge coincidence that Damian looked exactly like the stranger visiting the castle in her dreams.

"Hi."

Damian walked into the room wearing only a towel. His hair was damp and tousled; she'd never seen anything as sexy as he looked right now. Still she forced herself out of the bed, jumping a little as he smacked her rear as she walked back. When she scowled over her shoulder at him, he was grinning.

"Don't bother getting dressed when you're done," he said. "We're not leaving until we try that hot tub."

Jessi's shower was quick. She hurried from the steamy bathroom through the bedroom to find Damian reclining in the bubbling water. The fireplace was burning and the champagne flutes sat within easy reach as she joined him.

"Oh, this is heaven." She closed her eyes and let the warm, swirling water tease her naked skin. She felt Damian shift to her and relaxed against him. His body was becoming familiar. She felt at home in his arms, at ease whatever they did. She sighed and let her head drop against his shoulder. Her remaining pent-up stress and worry dissipated; nothing existed but the two of them.

"I love you," she said.

"Not half as much as I love you." She opened her eyes to meet his dark, serious gaze. "I've been indulging this strangers fantasy of yours, but I missed saying that.

I've missed you. I've missed this."

His lips touched hers tenderly, as if she was delicate and precious. She stroked his face, ran her fingertips along the scar, memorized the feel of his stubbled jaw. A few more days and he would be gone. A few more days and she'd return to the life that had seemed to be all she needed until he'd appeared at the airport.

As if by prearrangement, both the bubbling water and the fireplace stopped. The timers shutting off were like an alarm clock, reminding her that her mother was waiting at home and a full day lay ahead of her. Before she could get out, Damian pulled her on top of him, wrapped his arms around her waist and said, "Your mother would understand."

Damn. She'd forgotten to guard her thoughts. Next time someone created a lover for her, they could leave off the psychic stuff.

"Maybe, but I don't get home as much as I'd like. She enjoys having someone else in the house, someone to fuss over. "

"And you like being fussed over."

"Okay, I do." She kissed him lightly and pushed

against his arms until he let her go. She stepped out of the tub and grabbed her towel. Hastily drying off the worst of the wetness, she retreated to the bedroom and finished. She was nearly dressed by the time Damian joined her.

"Thank you," she said.

"For what?"

"For this evening. For reminding me there's more to life than work."

Before he could say a word in response, she slipped off to the bathroom. The noise of the hair dryer blocked her from hearing anything but its roar and by the time she was done, Damian was dressed and placing the champagne bottle back into its bucket.

"We'd better go before the coach turns back into a pumpkin," he said.

The sultry night air enveloped them as they walked hand in hand back to the car. Within moments, the air conditioner in the rental sedan was streaming chilled air over them. That, Jessi decided, defined her life at the moment perfectly: Hot and cold.

****

"Do we have everything?" Molly peeked into the

boxes and baskets on the table.

"If you take more, we'll need a bigger room." Jessi picked up a box and started carrying it to her mother's sedan. She'd planned week-long conferences that took less work than this shower for Becky. This morning they were decorating the church fellowship hall for tonight's event. This afternoon they were doing the last minute foods and tonight half the women in town would be there to celebrate the upcoming nuptials.

Damian helped load the trunk and waved goodbye as they backed out of the driveway and toward the church. Jessi almost felt sorry for him. Her cousin had ordered Tim and his friends to pick up Damian and show him a good time. Knowing that Tim's idea of a good time could range from hitting shots at the driving range to fishing, it was hard to tell what Damian end up doing.

All thoughts of everything but the shower disappeared after her aunt and an entourage of cousins showed up. She found herself standing on a chair holding one end of a banner while her mother yelled "Up!" or "Down!" at Jessi or her cousin Leigh, who held the other end. Every table had to be covered with hot pink or electric blue plastic cloths and set just so. Whether her aunt had found so many identical candy dishes she didn't know, but each one had to be filled with an equal amount of party mints in pink and yellow.

She was relieved when she and her much older cousin Dotty were assigned to go outside and line the sidewalk with multi-colored pinwheels. Anything was better than standing in the middle of crazy and waiting for the next order.

"We're doing this why?" she asked. "Everyone knows where the fellowship hall is."

"Because pinwheels were on sale and they thought Becky would find them whimsical." Dotty took one side of the walk, Jessi the other, as they placed the whirling toys exactly two feet apart.

"I assume we're also playing games."

Dotty nodded. "Oh, just wait. By the time this thing is over, we'll all be begging for mercy."

By mid-afternoon Jessi wasn't sure she'd survive until the shower even began. She hadn't seen this drill sergeant side of her mother before. While Damian was out doing whatever Tim had dragged him to, she sat at the kitchen table making sandwiches under her mom's eagle eye.

"Trim those crusts a little closer," Molly said, frowning at the egg salad creations underway. "There shouldn't be any sign of brown. And don't be stingy on the egg salad. I won't have anyone criticizing our refreshments."

Once the crusts were suitably cut, Jessi cut each sandwich into four perfect triangles which her mother arranged on a silver tray covered with a paper doily. By the time she'd made a similar number of tiny ham salad and tuna salad tea sandwiches, both Jessi's fingers and eyes ached. But the sandwiches did look perfect, which seemed to be her mother's only goal.

"Time for tarts," her mother said when Jessi stood up. "These are going to be such a hit."

Jessi sat back down. Soon she was filling small puff pastries with cheesecake filling and topping them with plops of cherry pie filling. A lesson in shaving chocolate and she soon had two trays of the small desserts ready to go.

"A little more chocolate on this one," her mother said as she inspected. Jessi obliged and felt a surge of triumph when her mother pronounced them suitable. She still didn't know why they couldn't have gone with a big sub sandwich cut into chunk, a bag of potato chips and a store-bought sheet cake. Except, of course, this was Durkin where "good enough" was never quite good enough.

She wasn't surprised when Damian followed them to the fellowship hall. He had been designated as the lifter and toter by her mother. She was quite pleased when he didn't dissolve in smoke the second he entered the building. Magical creature, maybe; demonic one, no. That was definitely reassuring after what they'd done together the last two nights.

"Whoa, girl, you have outdone yourself." Leigh stopped filling punch cups with ice to admire Damian. "If that's what you get by moving away, I'm turning in my resignation at the bank tomorrow."

The comments were getting old by the time Damian had made his fourth or fifth trip from the car to the kitchen. Yes, he was gorgeous. Yes, there were no men like him in Durkin. Jessi could readily agree to both those sentiments. The trouble was the pesky questions like how they met and when they were getting married. She thought about telling the truth, that they had no past and there wouldn't be a future either, but she knew nobody would believe her.

Becky's arrival was a godsend. All the aunties and cousins who had been conducting their inquisition of Jessi turned all their attention to the bride-to-be. By the time everyone had settled down and the shower began, he was gone. Jessi relaxed and allowed herself to get into the mood of things.

"Did I win?" she demanded after using rolls of bathroom tissue to create a wedding gown on Becky.

"Don't get in a hurry!" Dotty called back. Jessi cautioned Becky to stand still as the designated judges walked the line, considering Becky and the newest wives in the group, all of whom wore the same delicate tissue garb. Jessi knew she'd lost a few points for speed, since she was the last one done, but she was proud of the bows on her cousin's arms and the wad on her head that was supposed to be a veil.

She cheered when Dotty pronounced her the best designer and handed her a gift to open. Jessi tore off the paper, showed everyone the set of measuring cups inside and promptly handed them to Becky.

After a word game to see who could make the

most words from "honeymoon", Jessi sat beside Becky while she opened her gifts. She hadn't realized that among her duties as maid of honor was recording who gave what, but she was up to the task. She tried to keep her handwriting legible as she jotted "toaster oven" inside the card from Aunt Louise and "square casserole" inside the card from the pastor's wife. What seemed like a hundred years and severe finger cramps later, the guests descended upon the food her mother and aunts had made like starving locusts. Watching them, Jessi wondered why she'd had to trim off all those stupid crusts. No one even looked at the sandwiches before wolfing them down.

She was dead tired by the time the fellowship hall was restored to order and everything that needed to be taken home was packed in the car. Damian's rental car was in the drive when they arrived back at the house but he didn't answer when she called his name. Whatever adventure Tim had taken him on, it apparently wasn't over yet. So when her mother suggested that she let her take care of things and lie down for a bit, Jessi didn't object.

"I'm sure you're tired after today and all the

bowling you and Damian have been doing."

Jessi was so glad her mother was rinsing out dishes at the sink, her back to the room. If Mom had seen the blush she felt warming her face, no way could she have kept their nightly activities secret. She'd never been a good liar; even a frown from her mother had confessing immediately. Many things had changed since she left home, but not that.

"Are you sure?" she asked in a token protest.

"Positive." Molly turned and smiled. "Do you need me to tuck you in and read a bedtime story? You used to love that one about the handsome prince and the castle."

"I'm good." Jessi kissed her mother on the cheek. "Just don't let me sleep too long."

"Don't worry, dear, I won't. Now go on up to your room."

The blinds covering her bedroom windows kept the afternoon sun out. The welcome coolness of the air conditioning led her to slip under the chenille bedspread in her undies. Within minutes, she was asleep.

She watched the visitor with wary eyes. There

was such an intensity about him; she could not decide whether he truly came to see her father or if he was spying on the keep. There could be no better time to attack than when only a handful of soldiers defended the castle and the lands. A shiver ran down her spine at the thought of those she loved dead and the only home she'd ever known in the hands of another.

"Isobel!" She started at the sound of her name. The chief guard motioned her to join them. She joined them and agreed with a murmur when asked to prepare a room for their guest. Her father, she knew, would put this man in a room far from her. He was protective, perhaps too much so. She intended to have him near her own chamber and she would not sleep this night. Vigilance was called for.

The man was at the maid's table, eating a cold meal, when she sought him to show him the way to his temporary abode. She hesitated at the doorway. Being alone with a man didn't concern her; being alone with this one did.

"Join me." He swallowed before he spoke which meant he had some manners. His voice sounded educated, without the rough accent of most of the *people. Yet he did not come with escorts as another lord would have.*

"I have eaten well," she said.

"You would refuse a lonely traveler your company?"

She felt a blush rise. Her father would be ashamed of her rudeness. He was known for his hospitality and while he was away, she acted in his stead. She took the seat across from him, all too aware of his presence.

"You are a most unusual woman, you know."

She tipped her head and raised a curious eyebrow. "How so, sir?"

"You stand as boldly as any man demanding to know how I am and, I am certain, my intentions. Your own guard tells me that you have skills with weapons and that you are as respected as your father for your guidance and opinions."

"I am only as he has trained me," she demurred. "Did he also tell you that I have skill with a needle, am trained in medicinal herbs and control my own army of maids and cooks?"

He laughed. The rich sound resonated in her,

again bringing that strange longing. She stood and placed her hands on the back of her chair. He took the last bite of bread and cheese and swallowed.

"Tis growing late," she said. "I shall show you to your room."

He nodded and rose. She was overly conscious of his lean build and strong arms, filled with an aching wonder on how it would feel to be held in those arms, pressed against that body. Scolding herself for such ribald ideas, she led the way through the great room and up the steps to the long corridor upon which the family rooms opened. She went two doors past her own and said, "I hope this pleases you."

The man sighed. "I have slept so long on the ground that to sleep upon a bed again is an unimaginable pleasure. Sleep well."

"And you."

She should have stepped away. She should have run to her own room, away from that man who drew her so. Instead she swayed toward him in invitation, no better than the milkmaid who chased the boys who tended the barns. He drew her to him, his eyes questioning as he bent his head to kiss her.

Page 143

"Wake up, honey." The dream faded with her mother's voice, leaving Jessi filled with disappointment, even sadness. "Damian's back."

"Um, okay," Jessi mumbled, her voice thick with sleep. She fought to open her eyes. Her lips were dry and she had that fuzzy-headed feeling she usually got when she slept during the day.

"Jessi, did you hear me?"

"Yeah." She forced her eyes open. "I'm getting up."

Molly laughed. "I've heard that before. If you're not downstairs in five minutes, I'm coming up with a pan of cold water."

The full five minutes were up before Jessi managed to shake off her drowsiness and pull on capris and tee. The footsteps she heard on the stairs were too heavy for her mother; she was ready when Damian tucked his head inside the room and said, "I'm empty-handed."

"Then you can come in." She tipped her head and began brushing her hair, all too aware of how the air in the room seemed charged when he walked in and sat on the bed. Reality morphed into the remembered fantasy of her dream when he said, "Do you know how unusual you are?"

The traveler had said the same thing to Isobel, hadn't he? Or something like that. The smile on his face and light in his eyes were identical to her dream man's even though that was impossible. Had to be impossible.

"You think so?" She was pleased when her voice sounded solid.

"I know so. No one who's learned how to eat properly and handle angry clients would believe you would spend an hour tacking up banners and lining up pinwheels. Or that you saved the crusts you took off the sandwiches so you can feed the ducks at the lake later. Your mom told me that."

Jessi laid down the brush and ran her fingers through her hair. She had to remember that this guy didn't know her. No way was she the hard ass he described. Destinee could tell him that. Except, of course, Destinee saw her at her worst. Slamming her door shut after a broken appointment, griping about late-night flights, ordering her around as if Destinee was there only to jump and run when she said so. Damian

Page 145

was right. Even her trusted assistant and friend wouldn't expect to see her chucking bread to ducks.

But how did he know?

"Have I lost both of you?" At Molly's shout, Damian took Jessi's hand and led her out of the room and down the stairs. Two days ago, she wouldn't have let him do it. Today it felt perfectly natural. She was already used to the feel of his larger fingers clasped between hers, the pace of his walk, the little mannerisms lovers adored about each other. She was in way too deep. She loved him, her mother was ready to start knitting him his own Christmas stocking and her friends were drooling over how gorgeous he was.

And time was rushing by like flood water across a plain.

****

Fireflies lit the night as Jessi and Damian sat on the porch swing, gently rocking. Molly left right after dinner to help tie ribbons around the tiny bubble bottles that would be given to the guests right before the newlyweds left the church. Jessi had insisted on washing the dishes which became one more couples activity with Damian that she filed away for the long, lonely times after he disappeared. She'd washed and he'd dried despite his best efforts to convince her that air drying was healthier than using a dish towel. He also promised to take a look at Molly's leaking dishwasher the next morning to see if he could fix it.

Jessi was certain he could. So far there had been absolutely nothing the man couldn't do and do well in or out of bed. Especially in bed. The last two nights had been fantastic and she was certain he planned a repeat performance for tonight.

"Did you have a good time at the shower?" he asked.

Jessi nodded. "I love seeing my family. Every time I come home I swear I won't stay away as long again, but I do. How was your day with Tim?"

"Definitely interesting. Did you know he was a skeet shooting champion in high school?"

"Ah, so you went to the target range."

"There and to the hobby shop. Once he told me he made balsa wood models when he was a kid, I had to confess my own years of putting together plastic model cars. Then we challenged each other to a rocket shoot off."

Page 147

Jessi took her head from his shoulder and stared at him with disbelief. "You and Becky's redneck boyfriend shot off model rockets?"

"Yeah, out by a pond on Brent's farm. His old buddy and best man."

"I know Brent. He and Tim were the terrors of Durkin when they were about ten."

"That I can see. He's pretty much a big kid yet. Becky better be in charge of their checkbook."

"Oh, she will." Jessi laughed. "My cousin has a streak of sensible in her a mile wide although she'd never suspect it by the way she dresses and acts."

"Must run in the family."

Damian set the swing to rocking again. Jessi was content just to be with him. She reminded herself again that what was and what was to be didn't matter. For the first time in years, she was happy to simply live in the moment.

The serenity was interrupted by headlights playing across the porch as an SUV pulled into the driveway. Becky bounced out, followed more slowly by Tim who walked over to grab Damian's hand and pull him off the swing.

"My woman says we're going for ice cream," he said. "Don't bother to tell her you have plans. All you'll do is waste your breath and take a chance that they'll sell out of butter pecan before we get there."

They ordered their ice cream to go and headed out to the lake. The two couples walked hand in hand to an empty picnic table away from the beach. Tim brought a camping light out of the back of his vehicle to brighten the area.

"When's the last time you did this?" Becky demanded of Jessi.

"We came out here the other night."

"Not come to the lake. I meant kick back with friends. I bet you take a whole briefcase full of papers home every night, don't you?"

"Not every night." Jessi winced at how defensive she sounded.

"Most nights I bet." Becky turned to Damian. "You need to make her smell the roses and all that crap. She was a classic overachiever in high school and gotten worse once she left here."

Jessi waited to hear what her supposed boyfriend was about to say. Probably some cock and bull tale

Page 149

about how he whisked her away from her everyday dreariness on weekends for a trip to Paris or to go skiing in Switzerland to ensure her relaxation.

She was unprepared for him to reveal the truth, that she spent most nights in her apartment eating takeout with the television on to give the illusion of companionship. He glossed over the fact that he didn't exist by explaining that his work kept him on the road.

"You need to fix that," Becky scolded. "If you lose her, you'll be sorry."

"I already know that." Damian picked up Jessi's hand and kissed her palm. "Being here like this has been exactly what we needed."

Well, he hadn't lied. She'd needed a fiancé after Destinee's outrageous lie to her mother and he'd needed…to exist, she supposed. Once again she wondered what happened to him after everything wound down. Maybe like the magic genie, he'd hide away until someone else's wish was granted.

An irrational wave of jealousy swept through her as she thought of some other woman with Damian. She was, without question, losing it.

"Do you gabby women know it's almost

midnight?" Tim stood up and stretched. "You may get to sleep in tomorrow but I have to build an arch while my lady love picks up her dress. I've begged but she won't let me go with her."

"Because it's bad luck to see the bride before the wedding." Becky gave him a push. "Like you don't know that."

"I'm seeing you right now."

"But not when she's booootiful," Jessi teased. "She's going to be all tarted up and smell purty."

The ride back to the house was lively with laughter and teasing. Jessi's spirits were light as she waved goodbye to two of her favorite people in the world and walked up the front sidewalk. Damian stopped her before she could step onto the porch and, once Tim's tail lights had faded, pulled her tight and smiled down at her.

"Those are two great people," he said. "You're lucky."

Jessi knew that well. This town and these people had shaped her into the woman she'd become. Her success had come from the values instilled in her while she'd lived here in Michigan. She simply hadn't realized it until now.

Maybe that's why fate or whatever sent Damian to her. Seeing Durkin and her family through his eyes might be why he was here. Why they were together. What she needed to learn before he was gone forever.

"Thank you," she murmured.

"For what?"

"For being you. For being here. For helping me find myself."

"Hey, don't get all serious on me." He dropped a kiss on her cheek. "This is our vacation, remember?"

Our vacation. Oh, she loved the sound of that. And him.

"Are we going to stand out here and talk or doing something more, uh, interesting?" she asked.

Damian glanced at the house behind them. Only one window was lit, a living room table lamp gleaming at a low setting. Jessi wasn't surprised when he suggested they sneak into the house and her bedroom. Technically he'd only agreed not to come into her room, not vice versa. Still she knew the spirit of the rule.

"Come with me." She took his hand and made her way to the back yard. Although he stumbled once or twice in the darkness behind the house, she still remembered every bump and hole in the lawn. Like her bedroom, this hadn't changed since she'd moved away either. And as expected, the hammock hung between the two trees behind the garage. It had been a Father's Day gift to her dad but soon became her mother's favorite tanning spot. Wide and sturdy, it was plenty roomy for two.

Putting a finger to Damian's lips to keep him quiet, she wiggled his polo shirt off him before taking off her own tee. Next she kicked off her shoes and pulled off her capris, skimming her body against Damian's before she settled into the hammock. The snick of a zipper as he dropped his jeans and the sound of his leather shoes rubbing together when he slid them off let her know he understood perfectly.

He settled against her, fully naked. She arched her back for him to unhook her bra and raised her hips to let him slip off her panties. Skin against skin, her body merging with his, was once again perfect. So was the tenderness with which he held after they'd finished. She turned her head away from his chest so he wouldn't feel the salty warmth of her tears but stayed within the security of his embrace as she drifted off to sleep.

Chapter Eight

Jessi woke up alone in her bed with dawn barely breaking. Too much sleep; she realized she was full of energy and ready to get up. She vaguely remembered Damian carrying her to the back door and then their stealthy trip to their separate bedrooms. He'd kissed her in the hallway, that much she remembered. And handed over her clothes because they'd sneaked in stark naked.

She lay in bed and looked at the ceiling. What day was this anyway? She lived her life by a planner yet she wasn't sure if this was Thursday or Friday. She counted back mentally and realized today was the reunion picnic. Today all those girls who had been skinny and popular would see Jessi with her supposed fiancé. Life could be so sweet sometimes.

Her mother was still in bed so Jessi decided to surprise her by making breakfast. Humming under her breath, she checked out the refrigerator, freezer and cupboards. Everything she needed was there so she was soon chopping fruit and putting the frozen biscuits in the oven to bake.

Preoccupied with what she was doing, she didn't

hear footsteps behind her. When Damian said "Morning, beautiful," she jumped and gave a little shriek.

"You scared me half to death!"

"I'm glad I didn't kill you." He reached over and grabbed a strawberry from the dish. "I'm too hungry. Probably all that late night activity."

"Uh-huh." Jessi slapped his hand as he reached for another strawberry. "The coffee's ready. Maybe that will take the edge off."

Funny how his presence was unmistakable even when he was doing nothing more than sitting at the table. Comfortable was probably a better word, she decided. Being with Damian was comfortable.

Most of her childhood mornings had started much this way with her mother cooking and her dad watching as he enjoyed that first morning cup. She thought back over the few tentative relationships she'd had. She couldn't imagine a single one of those men sharing her kitchen. They were more of the six a.m. workout, early bird gets the worm mentality.

"Oh, honey, you shouldn't have." Molly's scolding greeting held a note of pleasure. She hugged Jessi before pouring coffee for herself.

"Hold off until you taste it," Jessi warned. "I haven't made sausage gravy in years."

Once again she ate like a longshoreman. Maybe it was the lack of stress or it could be from her nocturnal activities. She suspected the latter since she'd read somewhere that sex burned calories like crazy.

The cozy moment was interrupted by the ringing of her cell phone. She ran into the living room and dove for her purse.

"Hello?" she said, a bit breathless.

"Ooh, have I interrupted something?" Destinee replied.

"Just breakfast."

"Well, I'm disappointed. Your mom told me all about your gorgeous man so I hoped you were taking advantage of him."

"Why am I not surprised you two have been talking?"

"Oh, it's not like we're swapping details. You should be proud of your mother. She called to find out what I knew about lover boy."

If that was meant to boost her confidence, Jessi decided, those few words had the opposite effect. Her mother and her assistant had gotten her in this mess. She couldn't afford for anything to go wrong. Their appearance at the wedding and the reunion had to go without a hitch because if it didn't, her actions would live on in infamy. The collective memory of Durkin was long and thorough.

"Did you call for a reason or to make sure my food got cold?" Jessi tried to inject humor into the words.

"The crystal on your desk was cloudy today so I thought I should check on you. Seeing your aura would be better but that's a little hard."

"Especially since you're taking care of the office for me. The invoices need to be out by the first, remember."

"And I need to reconcile the accounts and verify your schedule for the next two weeks. I know, I know. That's not important now. I want you to promise you'll clarify your spirit before the day's end."

Jessi only half listened to the ritual Destinee described. The conversation from the kitchen served as a distraction as did the thought of her cooling breakfast. As soon as she could, Jessi ended the call. After assuring her mother nothing had happened, she settled back as Molly and Damian debated whether steaks were better grilled over charcoal or gas. Leaving them to their friendly disagreement, she took her last bite and headed for the shower. The hot water not only left her refreshed it also washed away any doubts Destinee's words had engendered. Cloudy crystal, her foot. She most definitely did not believe in that stuff.

Then what about Prince Charming?

"No, no, no." She stepped out of the shower and grabbed a towel. She'd done enough soul searching. Her plan to let things roll and hang on as best she could had worked well so far. There was no reason to change gears now. The moment. Concentrate on the moment.

"Get your butt down here!"

Heather's voice. Jessi dashed across the hall, pulled on summery shorts set and hurried down the stairs. She hugged her friend before asking if she wanted pancakes.

"No, I want to see The Dress. On you."

"You can see it at the wedding."

"Becky called and told me you were so beautiful she almost cried and that it fit you perfectly, no alternations needed. I want to see this piece of fashion heaven."

"So do we." Molly said. She and Damian joined them in the living room.

"Trust me, you do not."

The odds were against her. After all three ganged up on her and refused to change the subject, she raised her hands in mock surrender. Up the stairs she went once more. The dress looked even worse in the small confines of her bedroom under the overhead light. By wiggling, twisting and stretching her arm she managed to get the long back zipper all the way up and fasten the hook and eye at the nape of her neck. She adjusted the slippery fabric on her body and slid her feet into the dyed shoes. The feathery arrangement stayed in its box; she did not intend to keep that thing in her hair any longer than necessary.

She turned her head so she wouldn't see herself in the long mirror as she crossed her room. Once was enough. Blowing out a deep breath, she put her hand on the banister and attempted a glide down the steps and into the living room where her audience awaited.

Damian was the first to speak.

"Well," he said, "that dress is something."

"The color is quite cheerful," her mother added.

Heather busted out the truth.

"Oh, you poor thing, you look like a parakeet. I love you to death but yellow is seriously not your color. Please tell me you have a stole to wear at the reception to cover it up. Or a bathrobe. A long bathrobe."

The laughter underscoring Heather's words kept Jessi from taking offense. Everything she'd said was exactly what Jessi had thought. She leaned against the back of the recliner where Damian sat as her mother and supposed friend launched into a discussion of the appropriate makeup for such a gown.

"You do know they sell iridescent purple eye shadow, right? And green eye liner?" Jessi fluttered her eyelashes like a silent movie vamp. "I assure you I can create an effect that will have people talking longer after I leave."

Heather gave an evil grin. "And you know that I've been asked to be wedding photographer, don't you? I can ensure a video that gets more Internet hits than a dancing penguin."

When Jessi announced she was going up and

change, Heather followed. She lay on the bed as comfortably as her baby bump would allow as Jessi undressed and then redressed in her shorts and shirt. She chattered about her last doctor's visit and how she actually got Ryan to buy a suit for the reunion dinner-dance and the wedding. Finally she clumsily sat up and said, "Time for a little girl talk. Is your hot hunk of monkey love downstairs as good as he looks?"

"He's the perfect gentleman." Jessi decided to play dumb. "He also swims like an Olympic contender and bowls like a champion. Plus he even helped my mother dip strawberries."

Heather rolled her eyes. "That is not what I'm talking about. I want to do the down and dirty details. Sex, that's what I mean."

"Yes, his sex is male."

Heather threw a pillow at her. "I refuse to believe you two are not sleeping together. It's pretty obvious by the way you look at each other."

Jessi's eyes widened. If Heather thought so, her mother might have the same opinion. Oh, she'd die if her mother ever brought the subject up.

"Yes, he's good. Quite excellent, in fact."

"Please. Is it like daytime soap opera sex, cable sex or from one of those books we used to hide from our moms?"

"Nope. Done. End of discussion." Jessi tossed the pillow back onto the bed. "I am going downstairs now. Feel free to follow or if you'd rather you can snoop. He's sleeping across the hall."

"Are you kidding me?" The disappointment in Heather's voice was priceless. Jessi had no intention of telling her how little time he had actually spent in that bed.

"Enough about me," she said. "Let's talk about you. Boy or girl this time?"

"I have an ultrasound at my next appointment. Ryan says he doesn't care as long it's the last. Trust me, I agree. Four kids in ten years are plenty for anyone, even his mother who adores being a doting grandmother. His dad's just waiting for the day he can watch his grandson out on the football field and brag again about what a great quarterback Ryan was."

By the time they reached the living room, Heather was deep in an explanation about the new paint job she had planned for the nursery. Living in a big

Victorian meant plenty of room for the whole brood and Jessi was certain Heather loved every noisy moment of her life.

She did hear a note of excitement in her friend's voice as they talked about tonight's picnic and tomorrow's reunion itself. The social life of Durkin pretty much centered around whatever band was playing at the Elks Lodge and the various church fundraisers. The senior musical at the high school always sold out because it was as close to live theater as an audience could find here. Jessi wasn't so sure she was up to two nights with her old classmates. A few like her had left town for good after graduation or finishing college but most had stayed in the same general area. Durkin was not known for producing heart surgeons, noted judges or international bankers.

"You know this is a potluck, right?"

Jessi rolled her eyes at her friend's question. "Yes, I do."

"And you are planning to bring something a little more complicated than orange jello, I hope."

"Yeah, I thought I'd mix a box of orange and a box of lemon and throw some crushed pineapple in as a surprise."

"She's kidding, right?" This time Heather's question was directed to Molly.

"While she and Damian were out last night, I made a big bowl of my mustard potato salad and a chocolate cake. Don't worry. No one will get food poisoning from her contribution."

"Hey," Jessi protested. "I'm not that bad of a cook."

All eyes turned to her in disbelief. She gave up and admitted that the closest she's come to actually cooking in the last few months was heating up frozen pizza bites in the oven. She had a dozen carryout menus and she wasn't afraid to use them.

The striking of the grandfather clock brought a gasp from Heather who grabbed her purse and hugged Jessi, promising to see her that night. When she'd gone, Jessi cast an inquisitive glance at her mother.

"Oh, honey, you've been gone too long," Molly said. "School lets out in fifteen minutes and she wants to get a good place in line. Her youngest is in the afternoon preschool and riding the bus makes him cry."

And there was another reminder that she was

better off just visiting Durkin than even thinking about ever living here again. She didn't even know that the public school offered a preschool program. Or that Heather, who broke a half-dozen hearts before she finally settled on Ryan, would be such a softie.

Her mother had always made her walk home from school, even if it was raining or freezing cold. Yes, she had a rain slicker and umbrella for the wet months and a huge winter jacket and boots for the snowy times, but she would have loved not to have to slosh through puddles or slush. But what she'd considered pure apathy back then might have been her mom's way of gently nudging her toward independence.

"I think we should go shopping."

Molly's abrupt announcement brought a screeching halt to Jessi's reminiscing. Her mother hated to shop. If she couldn't find what she needed at the dollar store downtown or the supermarket, she'd order online.

"As in go to the mall?" she asked.

"Exactly." Molly looked her daughter up and down. "You're presentable as long as you don't wear those ridiculous flip flops. Put on some decent shoes and let's go."

Jessi threw Damian a baffled glance; he shrugged. Still, his lack of protest at going shopping with two women made her wonder if he and her mother hadn't cooked something up. Something strange was going on indeed.

Stranger still was their destination. When her mother pulled into a parking space near the fanciest department store the area had to offer, alarms went off in Jessi's head. Her mother wasn't shopping for herself. She was dragging Jessi in to buy something.

Damian had chosen to sit in the back seat so Jessi and her mother could talk. He was out of the car in record time, opening Jessi's door for her and offering his hand. People passing by probably saw it as a nice gesture but they didn't know it was a way to keep her from escaping.

"This way." Marching with the determination of a drill sergeant, Molly led the way to what overhead sign declared to be Women's Special Occasion Dresses. Jessi would have attempted to dig her heels in and refuse to follow except that the floor was some smooth and highly waxed surface. Falling on her butt was not in her plans for the day.

"Destinee told me you were planning to wear a suit tomorrow."

"A very expensive suit that's appropriate for any occasion."

"Phooey." Molly pointed toward a rack of summer dresses. "If you have to be fancy-schmancy, you can at least be stylish."

When the sales clerk bore down on them, Jessi decided just to give up. Dealing with Mom was like facing a steam roller sometimes. You might as well surrender before getting smooshed flat.

The stream of dresses brought to her in the dressing room seemed unending, although she realized it was probably just six or seven. She marched out in each one to endure her mother's scrutiny. Damian was no help; he told her she looked beautiful in everything. Her mother was far less kind. One dress made her hips look wide, another was cut too low in front. One was too short, the next too long. Finally the clerk and her mother both agreed on the one dress Jessi might actually wear again, an ecru mid-calf dress with delicate embroidery at the hem.

Jessi tried to pay but her mother was faster with a credit card. When her mother suggested they look for shoes and a purse, she set her foot down.

"I brought a pair of sandals with heels that will be perfect," she said. "And you're not spending money on an evening bag. You still have that one with the gold sequins, don't you?"

She was surprised but relieved when her mother decided that might just do. In her own world of corporate events and mandatory social outings, she had two little black dresses and the accessories to go with them. That plus her suits were all she needed.

It was only a little after one but Jessi expected her mother to be ready to leave. Once again she was proved wrong. Instead of heading for the door that led back to the parking lot, Molly wove her way through the aisles to the wide opening into the mall itself. Jessi's stomach rumbled; she was ready for lunch. Her mother had other ideas.

"That dress needs something to set it off," she said. "A new necklace, maybe."

"Mom, I brought practically everything from my jewelry box with me."

Page 169

"Which I'm sure is fine for those damned suits of yours. You're a nice-looking woman now and you should make the most of it."

"Yes," Damian agreed, "please let me buy you something." He led the women toward a top-end jewelry store. "Consider it a remembrance of this week."

Oh, she didn't need a tangible possession for that. No way could she forget a single moment. Not the shock of seeing him at the airport, the incredible pleasure they'd found with each other, the easy way he fit in with her family and friends. She wouldn't even need photos, although she was going to make sure she took her camera to the weekend events. The wrath of Destinee would fall upon her if she came back without any, she was certain.

"The jewelry I brought will be fine. If you insist on spending money on me, let's go there." She pointed toward the food court. "I'm thirsty. And famished."

To her surprise he agreed. Before long she was biting into a corn dog while her mother and Damian shared a basket of chili cheese fries.

"Ummm." She dipped the tip of the corn dog into mustard and took another bite. She had no intention of abandoning the healthy eating she'd adopted since leaving home but one cheat wouldn't hurt. She told herself the same thing as she stole a fry. Sometimes a woman needed chili and gooey cheese to top off a day.

Or to prepare to face the other 57 graduates from her high school class. Her contact was casual, limited to occasional exchanges on Internet. Her mother was good for passing on the big news but Jessi had no idea who was married, who had divorced and who had gained enough weight or lost too much hair for her to recognize them.

"We've got to go." A quick look at her cell phone time had her on her feet and gathering up the trash. "I'd like to be unfashionably on time instead of fashionably late."

"There is no such thing as fashionably late in Durkin," her mother said to Damian. "If you're even two minutes late, you might as well go back home."

Jessi made sure they weren't even one minute late. Carrying the bowl of her mother's potato cake, she and Damian approached the covered tables at the lake shelter house at exactly seven minutes until six. Heather and Ryan were already there; as soon as she'd

Page 171

introduced the two men, Ryan led Damian away in search of a beer. Jessi wasn't surprised to see the other women's eyes following him. Damien was definitely the best-looking guy there.

Recognizing her classmates hadn't been as hard as she'd feared. Only looks had changed during the fifteen years since they'd crossed the stage at graduation. Voices, mannerisms and personalities were still the same. Before long she was deep into exchanging memories of favorite teachers, hated classes and all the times that made their high school years distinctively their own. She even forgot about Damian until he walked up and handed her a tall glass of something golden.

"Gin and lemonade," he said. "Heather said it was your drink of choice."

"Wow, I haven't had one of these for a long time." Jessi took a long sip. "I can't believe I forgot how much I like this."

"Remember how we'd take the lemonade and Jake Hansen brought the gin?" Heather plopped down beside her and wiggled her own glass. "Enjoy that. The baby and I are having caffeine-free soda."

The call came from their senior class president for everyone to get in line and eat. Jessi loaded her plate, unable to decide what not to take. All of her favorite foods were here from deviled eggs to pineapple upside-down cake. At the rate she was going, she'd have to fast for a week when she got home just to fit into her clothes.

She slapped Damian's hand when he tried to sneak a chicken wing off her plate, bringing chuckles from those sitting around her. It was hard for her to remember now why she didn't want come back for this. Her formative years, from kindergarten to graduation, had been spent with these people. They'd learned to ride bikes together, cheered themselves hoarse at basketball tournaments together, cried and laughed with each other.

"I am so glad you came." Heather squeezed Jessi's hand. "Do you how long it's been since we've goofed around?"

Yes. She most definitely did. Since before she decided to open her own business. Before she became so committed to hitting a self-imposed goal of X number of clients and Y amount of dollars. Before she realized how fleeting time is. She was grateful her eyes had been opened while her mother was still her vibrant self and before Heather and her other friends had given up on her.

As daylight waned, a few of the men lit the bonfire that had been built earlier in the day. Jessi leaned her back against Damian's front, his arms wrapped around her waist, to watch the pile ignite and flame. The air filled with the smell of burning wood and the crackle as the fire spread; laughter rose as well.

Her life was perfect. Jessi tipped her head back and smiled at Damian who dropped a kiss on her forehead in response. Her other life seemed so far away. Seizing the moment was definitely the way to go.

She wasn't too surprised when some of her classmates sat on the ground to watch the fire and other couples wandered off into the woods or that Damian tugged her away from the group too. She giggled as he used his cell phone to light the way down a path that hadn't been taken by the others. When they reached a clear spot with a fallen log, he made a show of brushing off the worst of the bark and debris. He offered her a seat with a bow and a sweep of his hand. Jessi gave an imaginary curtsey and sat down. Damian took his place beside her.

"You're different tonight." He brushed a stray hair off her cheek.

"It's like I'm sixteen again."

"Sweet sixteen and never been kissed?"

"Kissed, yes. More than that, no."

"Kissed like this?" His lips touched hers, soft and tasting of baked beans and mustard.

"Umm." She smiled up at him when he pulled away. "That was so much better."

He smiled back and slid his arm around her shoulders. She cuddled against him; contentment filled her. She'd forgotten the sound of the bullfrogs that lined the lake, the way sound carried on a still night. It felt as though they were the only two people in the world but the singing coming from the bonfire and a conversation somewhere near them reminded her where they were.

Jessi listened more closely to the tune wafting to them. Their high school fight song, which was the same as it been in her mother's day and probably would be same when everyone in her class was old and gray. She sang along softly without realizing she was doing so.

"You have a nice voice."

"Proudly stood in the back row of the alto

section."

"What, no solos?"

"Not hardly. Nor was I ever chosen for first chair clarinet."

"I didn't know you were in the band."

"Orchestra. We were truly elegant in button-down white shirts and burgundy velvet skirts. Long velvet skirts."

"Sounds sexy."

"Oh, yeah. Guys love girls who play the clarinet and have to be in by 10 p.m."

"Well, good girl, maybe we better go back and join the others. I don't want your mom to find out we've been in the woods alone."

Shouts of "Come on!" and "We know what you've been doing!" greeted them as they rejoined the group at the fire. Ryan grabbed Damian to find another beer while Jessi found Heather sitting at a picnic table. Several other women joined them and they were soon comparing notes of their lives now and what they'd predicted them to be in their class prophecy. She was relieved that she wasn't the only one who hadn't lived up to the expectations of the graduating class.

"I know all I talked about was being a nurse, but I can't imagine that now," commented one of them.

"What are you doing now?" Jessi asked.

"International corporate law. I spent three years in Switzerland and two in France before I decided it was time to come back to the States. I'm with a firm in Washington D.C. now."

"Excuse me, but no boring talk." Heather waved her glass. "What I really want to know is if Frenchmen pinch you the way I've heard."

Jessi joined in the wave of laughter that followed. She was content to let the conversation flow around her. Any worries she had about feeling like a stranger had long ago melted away along with the years. She'd told Damian the truth: She felt like the teenager she'd professed to be, crazy about the boy she was with and afraid a break-up was coming any time. Which was close enough to the truth for her to shove it way to the back of her mind.

The dying of the bonfire served as a cue for the group to split up with promise of seeing each other the next night for the main event. Jessi thought it was sweet how couples who had walked up to the picnic tables with a foot or two of space between them were holding hands or leaving with their arms around each other. She wasn't the only way who felt time regress, it seemed.

Damian handed her keys when they reached the car. She'd only had that one alcoholic drink while he'd consumed several long necks. The fact that he hadn't asked her if she minded was either responsible behavior on his part or the impossibility of him doing anything wrong. She preferred option one.

Her mother's presence on the porch when they arrived home surprised her. She figured everything was okay since Mom was settled into her favorite chair with votive candles lit on the small table beside her. A light breeze brushed against her as they walked across the dewy lawn, carrying with it the fragrance from a neighbor's flowers.

"Have a good time?" Molly asked.

"Yes, ma'am," Damian replied. "I know we're a little past your daughter's curfew but I assure you Jessica wasn't getting into trouble.

"That's good. I'd hate to have to call your parents." Molly blew out the candles and stood. "I'll leave you two to say good night. Remember, Jessi, I'll be right inside the door."

After the door shut, Jessi said softly, "So does this mean we're not bowling tonight?"

"Jessica Flint, you are such a hussy."

His use of the old-fashioned word tickled her. That so much nicer than slut or skank, the words bandied about these days. These days. Now she was the one who seemed old.

"I take that for a no." She rose on her tiptoes and dropped a kiss on his cheek. "Now I better get inside before my mother grounds me."

She left the door open behind her, knowing Damian would be right behind her. Tonight they would both go to their respective rooms, go to bed and stay there. The mood the picnic had created still held her in its thrall.

Chapter Nine

She expected his kiss. Instead his lips stopped tantalizing close and he whispered, "You tempt me greatly, my lady. But I will not repay your father by compromising his most precious possession."

Tears welled; she turned her head and blinked them back. He had refused her yet his arms still held her. She felt his hardness against her leg and knew it was not lack of desire that stayed him. Rough though he appeared, this was truly a gentleman.

"I do not even know your name." The hot breath of his words touched her skin and brought a shiver.

"Isobella DeFaye. And you are?"

"Daelfin of Falconwerth."

She knew little of the village of Falconwerth save that it produced some of the king's finest soldiers, or so her father once said. It lay far beyond the wooded hills, too far for one such as she to ever expect to travel. Were all men of that far town like this one? she wondered, strongly built and fair in appearance. Soon, she knew, she would be wed to a man of her father's choosing. Suitors had already come to seek her hand but her father had seen their purpose. They were interested more in becoming the next lord of this estate and less in taking a wife.

She could not expect to marry for love. That was the stuff of tales. She did hope the man with whom she would spend the rest of her years was intelligent and would accept her speaking her own mind. Father and she had spent many a winter night in lively debate. If she were reduced to supervising servants and serving only as a brood cow for some old man, she would prefer to retire to a nunnery for her remaining days.

She met this man's eyes boldly once again.

"Tell me, Daelfin of Falconwerth, do you intend to release me this night or shall we stand like thus until the cock crows?"

His arms dropped instantly and he stepped back. The tension that had filled her body with his touch remained; she feared it would torment her still after she was in her bed. His touch was gentle as he stroked her hair only once, as if unable to stop himself.

"A thousand apologies, my lady." He bowed. "You need not bar your door. I will not step across this threshold until the daylight comes."

Page 181

He walked into the room she'd given him, pulling the door shut tight behind him. Isobel sagged against the wall. Her legs seemed to quiver and a queer throbbing filled her. This fascinating stranger could so easily overcome her training and common sense. Once again she vowed to sleep not but to keep watch in her father's stead.

Jessi woke with a start. Her mouth was dry as cotton and her eyes were thick with sleep. She glanced at the alarm clock. Just a bit after two. She seldom woke in the night. Once asleep she stayed asleep until something or someone woke her. She had a nagging feeling, though, that she needed to be awake. But why?

She punched the pillow, turned on her other side and ordered herself to go to sleep. Instead she grew wider awake and finally gave up. She padded downstairs barefoot and went into the kitchen. She was probably hungry. She hadn't eaten much at the potluck and her lunch of a corn dog and root beer probably didn't even count as food.

Unlike her own, her mother's refrigerator had treasures on every shelf. Jessi held the door open and stared inside as the cool air poured out to her. Cold chicken or ham sandwich? Some more of her mom's potato salad or a pudding cup? She finally decided on all of them. She slathered mayonnaise and mustard on the bread which encased two slices of thick ham and put it on a plate. Next to it she placed a chicken leg, a big spoonful of potato salad and grabbed two of the little butterscotch pudding containers. If she was going to have a midnight feast, she intended to do it right.

The street was quiet around her as she opened the front door with her elbow and stepped onto the porch. Durkin was one of those places where no one locked their doors which made sneaking in and out much easier. Not that she was sneaking exactly. She was celebrating a little time alone.

The food was heavenly. Jessi demolished the sandwich quickly before biting into the chicken. She made a mental note to find out how her mom seasoned it. As far as she was concerned, it was even better than the famous chain's offerings.

Once the potato salad was gone, she put the pudding aside for dessert in a little while. Sitting here looking up at the stars was a treat in itself. The stars shone over the city, sure, but she never saw them. Street lights, layers of neon and a layer of pollution let only the brightest share their light.

The moon was full, she realized. Luckily Durkin had no werewolves, as far as she knew, so she felt comfortable leaving the porch to walk around the block. Lawns glistened with dew and solar lights gave a reassuring glow along some sidewalks and flower beds. She noticed that most of the cars in the driveways were SUVs. Back when she was a kid, station wagons were the must-have. She tried to remember if car manufacturers even made them anymore.

Her pudding cups were right where she left them. She curled back onto the swing, picked up her spoon and dug into the first one. It was creamy, sweet and the perfect complement to her nostalgic mood.

Two more days with family and friends and her time here was over. Mom would take her to the airport in Detroit, hug her goodbye and this idyll would end. She'd go back to the office and on to wherever her business took her and Damian would disappear.

The very thought was like salt in a wound. She couldn't bear not looking into those deep, sensual eyes again. Didn't think she could live without being held by him or listening to his laugh. She ought to fire Destinee for this.

Or maybe thank her. There was no question now. Damian St. Clair was the man from her dreams. Although the details soon slid away, each left her with a clearer picture of the stranger in her father's castle. Each made her surer it was the man who now slept upstairs.

"Damn." She shoved the spoon into the half-eaten cup and looked at the sky. Her dad had told her when she was a kid that the man in the moon would grant her wishes if she just believed hard enough. She'd never gotten the pony she'd longed but she had received an invitation to prom from Danny Parker after wishing on the moon. Staring at the orb overhead, she made a spontaneous request.

"Let him be real," she asked the moon. "Don't let this be all there is."

The man in the moon didn't even wink. Sighing and feeling a little silly, she picked up the remains of her impromptu meal and went back into the house. She rinsed her plate and spoon, threw away the empty cup and went back upstairs. Maybe with her stomach full

Page 185

she'd sleep again.

Jessi was shocked awake, certain someone had called her. There was a name for that phenomenon; she'd read it somewhere. Being jolted awake didn't lead to lingering in bed. She took a quick shower and dressed. Tonight was the reunion; tomorrow was the wedding. And then…

Rather than make her time her enemy, she decided to embrace it. She would not waste one minute with Damian. Certainly her mother would understand.

They were both on the porch with their morning coffee when she came downstairs. Her mother looked tired. Damian looked magnificent, of course, even in a polo and khakis.

"I thought we'd go to the historic village today," Jessi said. "All of us."

"You two go without me," Molly begged off. "I promised to make molded chocolate roses for the tables at the reception."

"Would you like me to stay and help?"

"Oh, heavens no." Her mother made a shooing motion with her hand. "You kids need to have a little fun. Don't forget that little restaurant on the way. They have the best lemon meringue pie."

The weather couldn't have been better if Jessi had ordered it. There was enough breeze to counteract the July sun and no hint of rain in sight. The quaint village was a mixture of old and reconstructed buildings and they held hands as they wandered from one to another. Jessi snapped a picture of Damian in the stocks on the common yard by the church; he returned the favor and took one of her. An accommodating stranger took over the camera as they posed by the blacksmith's shop.

"You are a beautiful couple," the woman complimented as she handed the camera back.

And a temporary one.

Jessi could almost feel the minutes rush by. Before long they'd have to go back to Durkin and get ready for the reunion. That time would disappear and dawn come again. One final day and then a forever without him.

"Hey, quit looking so serious." Damian swiped a finger down her nose.

"I was trying to remember where that restaurant

is," she lied. "Mom will expect a report when we get home. In case you hadn't noticed, my mother is a serious foodie."

"No!" Damian faked shock. "You mean she doesn't see chicken nuggets as gourmet food?"

His good humor chased away the cloud that had begun to form over Jessi. They wandered through the gift shop, where she bought a cookbook for her mother and a book of Indian legends for Destinee. The clerk gave perfect directions to the restaurant which proved to still have the same excellent cuisine.

"Oh, and a piece of lemon meringue pie to go," Damian said as the waitress brought the bill. Jessi wasn't at all surprised that he was taking the dessert to her mother. She would have expected nothing less.

She was content on the ride home to listen to the radio and enjoy Damian's company. His hand was warm on her thigh and every so often, he'd give her a look that assured her he had no intentions of being prim and proper tonight. Nor did she. This was, after all, their last night together.

As if he'd read her thoughts – and maybe he had – Damian said, "I talked to your mother this morning before I made reservations for the suite again. She's not expecting us home until morning."

Jessi grinned, elated at the thought of spending the whole night together, of actually falling asleep in his arms and waking up with him still beside her. Now she wanted time to fly, for the evening's festivities to be over so they could be alone.

****

"Do you think it's too late to pay them to elope?"

Molly stood at the kitchen counter, surveying her creations with a critical eye. She'd tinted white chocolate so that there would be a long-stemmed red rose with green leaves and stem at each table. She'd also molded rose buds in a variety of colors from pale yellow to Becky's favorite orange, red and purple.

"They look great, Mom."

Molly rolled her eyes. "You have to say that because you're my daughter. I'm not happy at all with that blue and some of the leaves are thinner than others for some reason. I just hope nobody looks too close at them."

"Forget about the candy and eat your pie." Jessi pulled the takeout box from the refrigerator. Ryan had come by and picked up Damian for some mysterious errand, leaving the two women alone. Jessi knew how frazzled the wedding preparations were making her mother. A little time doing nothing might calm her nerves.

"Remember your grandmother's rhubarb pie?" Molly asked as they sat at the table. "Her crust was every bit as good as this."

Jessi shivered. "Oh, but the filling was so bitter. I know she and Grandpa loved it that way but it puckered my mouth with every bite. She made great biscuits, though."

"And her raspberry jam. She gave me her recipe but it's not the same when I make it."

Once again Jessi was reminded how much Grandma was like her own mother. Grandma and Mom shared a kitchen with ease, falling into familiar patterns whenever they worked together. She'd never found that synchronicity. Helping with meals back in her teen year and even now, she hadn't been an equal to her mother. She'd been more an assistant. Mom had created the magic while Jessi had supplied the most basic of skills.

With Dad, though, things were different. He'd

taught her how to change the oil in the car, how to clean off the bottom of the mower deck and how to create a working budget. She'd been his shadow whenever she could. If he ran to the hardware store on Saturday, she tagged along. When he trimmed bushes, she carried off the trimmings to the backyard burn pile.

"Did you ever wish I did stuff more with you?" Jessi asked when her mother paused.

"You have a busy life."

"No. When I was a kid. I tagged after Dad everywhere and we left you alone."

"You needed that time with your father." Molly took her last bite of pie. "After his heart attack, the one thing I was grateful for was that you had spent so many hours together. Some men are disappointed because they don't have a son but your dad thought the sun rose and set because of you. I always figured that when once you got married and had kids, I would start getting emergency calls day and night."

"That could still happen."

"Oh, I hope so." Molly's face took on a glow. "I know all that old stuff isn't supposed to be used any more but your crib, play pen and high chair are still up in the attic. It's silly but I've even thought about painting the spare room a nice yellow. With those windows, it would be a nice children's room for when you bring the kids to visit."

"Oh, Mom. That sounds marvelous."

"Now that you've met Damian, maybe I ought to start pricing paint." With that pronouncement she stood and carried her plate to the sink. The running water as she rinsed it, back to her daughter, was a message that she was done with that subject.

"Hadn't you better start getting ready?" she asked after turning the water off.

Jessi glanced at the clock above the sink. Her mother was right. Since apparently tonight's reunion was a big deal, she'd need extra time to do her hair and put on make-up. There was still plenty of time for a leisurely bath, however.

"Ah!" The shriek came involuntarily she stepped from the hot and steamy bathroom into the hall and ran into Damian. She held her towel tighter and smiled as he stepped back, his hands thrown up in apology.

"You scared me. I didn't expect you there."

"I'll make up for it. Later." He dropped a kiss on her cheek, then her shoulder. "Umm, you smell good."

"Thank you, kind sir." She tried the best curtsey she could in her towel. "All part of my master plan."

"Master plan?"

"To make sure this is a night you'll never forget." She slid past him and into her room, shutting the door behind her. Anticipation bubbled as she rubbed on body lotion. The new dress didn't seem like such a waste of money now. She pulled on her sexiest underwear and bra and opened her jewelry case. Holding up one piece after another against the dress, she finally decided on a simple gold chain and hoop earrings. Simplicity had its virtues.

A quick blow-drying, some work with a curling iron and Jessi was satisfied with her hair for once. She decided on a subtle approach with her makeup, using natural colors on her eyes instead of brighter eye shadow and multiple coats of mascara. She wasn't trying to impress anyone. She wanted to be beautiful for Damian. As beautiful as possible, anyway.

She heard the door across the hall open as she was strapping on her shoes. She waited until Damian had time to get downstairs before she started down the steps. If this was the equivalent of a senior prom years after the real event, she intended to make the same kind of entrance for her date again.

Her dramatic entrance lost a little of its punch when she caught her heel on the carpet of a lower step. She stumbled but regained her balance in time to step into the foyer with a sweep worthy of an old-school movie starlet, bringing applause from her mother and a whistle of appreciation from Damian.

"Oh, let me get my camera," her mother said, rushing to the desk drawer where it was kept. Jessi offered an "I'm sorry about this" smile to Damian who walked over to pose beside her.

"Don't stand there like bumps on a log." Molly snapped her fingers and pointed at her supposed son-in-law to be. "Put your arm around her, hug her, do something."

Jessi was shocked when he grabbed her around the waist and lifted her. She gasped when he swung her in a big circle, laughter bubbling over when he set her back down. She leaned against him and looked into his smiling eyes.

Page 194

"Perfect." Molly hit the button to review the digital shots. "I can't wait to share these."

"Let me see," Jessi demanded.

"Later. You two need to be on your way."

Damian handed Jessi her borrowed evening bag and told her to wait a moment. He disappeared into the kitchen and returned with what she recognized as a florist's box. Opening it, he presented her with a wrist corsage of yellow daisies and other small flowers she didn't recognize.

"Oh, wow." Jessi slipped the elastic of the corsage over her hand. "I can't remember the last time I wore flowers when I went out."

Excitement she hadn't expected filled her as they pulled into the lot of the country club. She recognized Heather's mini-van and some of the other vehicles from last night but she knew there would be others here who hadn't made the picnic. Her chemistry lab partner was one of them. She knew he'd left town, too, and heard he had married. Since he was probably the smartest guy Durkin High had produced, she'd love to know what he was doing now.

They stopped to check in at the long table just

outside the entrance to the club's ballroom. Music she'd listened to over and over during her teen years played inside the room which was already filled with a number of chattering people. She was relieved to see that the name badges had pictures from their senior yearbook. She was far more apt to recognize people as they'd been than as they were now.

"Oh my gosh, Jessi, you made it." She didn't have to see a name tag to know Amy was grabbing her in a big hug. Just because she hadn't seen her band mate in ten years didn't mean she'd forgotten her. Sitting next to someone for four years cements a friendship.

John, her lab partner had shown up, she soon saw. April, his obviously pregnant wife, was not only pretty and charming but also a molecular biologist, she soon found out.

"We met at an innovation conference," April said, casting a fond glance toward her husband. "He and I served on a panel on the pros and cons of genetic-engineered food and ended up sitting in the hotel bar talking for two hours afterwards."

In the flurry of catching up, Jessi ended up separated from Damian. Finally looking around for him, hoping he wasn't bored to death, she spotted him standing with a group of men that she suspected were also escorts of alumni. He smiled and waved, reassuring her that things were fine.

The night couldn't have been better. The prime rib dinner was excellent; the band played the perfect music for dancing. She laughed until tears came watching the former cheerleaders try to recreate one of their old routines and cheered when the last prom king and queen were called up to receive new crowns.

Still she wasn't reluctant to leave. The best part of the night was yet to come.

****

Champagne and chocolate were waiting in the room again. Bouquets of flowers helped create an aura of romance with bright bunches on the table and the mantel above the fireplace, even rose petals scattered around the hot tub. Damian pulled off his suit jacket and tie and tossed them onto the couch as soon as they closed the door. Meeting her eyes and holding her gaze, he undid the top two buttons of his shirt and rolled up the sleeves. Jessi responded by kicking off her shoes and sliding off the wrist corsage. Damian's shoes came off;

so did her earrings.

Before he took did any more undressing, Damian crossed over, opened the champagne and filled two flutes. He pressed the remote control for the fireplace. It sprang into blazing life. Another push on the controller and soft orchestra music filled the room.

Jessi accepted the sparkling wine and settled into the couch.

"On with the show," she encouraged him.

"Your wish is my command."

"As it should be."

Damian answered with the sexy smile she loved and a slow unbuttoning of his shirt. He stopped, sipped his drink and then unzipped his suit pants just enough to pull out his shirt tail and strip off the white cotton garment.

"More," Jessi requested as she waved her glass toward him.

"More me or more champagne?"

"Both."

He accommodated. She sipped until he stood before her with his fingers at the waistband of his black silk boxers. Proof of his desire jutted before her.

"My turn." She beckoned him to her and slid the smooth fabric down his thighs and his calves, sighing as he kicked them away. "Very nice view."

"I know a better one." Damian pulled her to her feet. His hands went to her back and slid down the zipper. The fabric fell and pooled on the floor. His fingers worked the clasp of her lacy bra before pushing the straps off her shoulders and down her arms.

When she was naked too he led her to the bubbling spa. Damian stepped in; he pulled her atop him when she followed. The hot water swirled around her, across her, teasing her already aroused body. His now-familiar kisses and tantalizing touch took away thoughts of anything but this moment and this man. Growing passion led her to forget that she intended to remember every detail. She could only feel and react, tension growing and easing inside her as Damian employed his skillful touch to keep from exploding until he wanted.

Finally she could take no more. She settled herself on him. Linking hands with him she moved on his hard rod, taking pleasure in his gasps. When he reached release she let herself go as well, deep moans exploding from her. She loved this man. Dear God, how she loved him.

The shouting from Daelfin's room had Isobel on her feet, grabbing her dagger and running across the hall. She had promised him safety; if he was under attack, she would kill the traitor herself. She rushed into the room with her blade uplifted only to discover that the ruckus was created by the visitor himself. He thrashed upon the bed, his limbs battling the bedcovers while his cries echoed against the walls. Isobel hesitated, torn between waking him to end the torment and fear that to wake him would worsen things. She called his name, softly at first and then with force, but with no response.

The guards were on the other side of the castle near the great hall. Their position allowed for the strongest defense but she longed for some, even one, to be near enough that a call would bring them to her. This Daelfen of Falconwerth was a strong man with a warrior's skills and could overtake her before she could take another breath. Could, she reminded herself. Not would.

Gathering her courage, she hurried to the bed

and grabbed his shoulders. He flinched upward, nearly pulling her off her feet. She dug her fingers into his flesh and screamed his name. His body tensed and his eyes opened. She threw herself back as he lunged for her. Prepared for a fist's pound, she was taken aback when he wrapped his arms around her and sighed, "My beloved. You have come."

His lips came down on hers; his hands splayed across her back. Her shock receded as a rush of heat rolled through her and robbed her of her senses. He pulled her atop him before rolling over in a quick move to trap her beneath his body. She stared into eyes dark with desire, trembled as he slid a knee between her thighs and forced them open. Her fingers tangled in his hair as his mouth crushed against hers. He frightened her yet like a moth drawn to candlelight, she was unable to resist. Her body arched against his leg as he pressed into the delicate vee between her legs, a wild spasm coursing through her.

"I thought you were lost to me forever." His whisper was hot against her skin. "I watched you die yet you are here in my embrace."

The words came to Isobel in a fog. He was a

Page 201

stranger yet she felt as if she'd known him forever. She had never lain with a man but she knew his body intimately, from the hard muscles along his ribs to the scars on his back. She did not understand but neither did she care. This moment, this man, was all that mattered.

A vision came to her, almost a memory yet nothing she had experienced. The cottage was small, the bed only straw upon the floor with his cloak thrown over. Yet she desired nothing finer. She had needed only her husband and his love. These stolen moments when she could find a way to slip out sustained her, reminded her that one day the war would end and they could be together forever.

"I love you," Daelfen whispered as he entered her with great gentleness. "Promise you will never leave me again, my beautiful Fiona. Never."

Jessi woke with a shudder, her face wet with tears. This once was all they'd had. He had left her at daybreak, ridden hard to the west. He had vowed he would be back, swore he would ask her father for her hand. Then the word had come only days after she realized she carried his child.

"No." Her mouth formed the soundless word. She curled against the heat of Damian's body, her ear against her chest so she could hear his heartbeat. Even though he slept soundly, his arm came around her to hold her tight.

"Daelfen," she whispered against his skin. "I'll never leave you. Never."-

Chapter Ten

Jessi slammed her hand against the bedside table, trying for the snooze button. Her fingers felt flower petals and the thin stem of a goblet but the noise continued. Blinking, she peered at the stand and realized where she was. She was in bed with Damian who had grabbed his cell phone from the other stand beside him and was hitting the button to stop the 1812 Overture from blaring through the room.

"Tell me you don't wake up to that every day."

"I wanted something we wouldn't sleep through."

"Good choice."

He chuckled. "Want me to program it in your phone?"

"No. Definitely not."

A sharp knock came at the door of the suite. Damian slid out of bed, pulled on his pants and left the bedroom. Jessi heard him in conversation and then the door closing. Before she could get up to investigate, he was walking toward her with a tray of covered dishes. A single red rose in a silver vase decorated the tray.

"So this is why you made sure we were awake."

"Breakfast in bed is supposed to be romantic. I thought we'd see for ourselves."

"You know what would be even better? Breakfast by the fireplace."

The time passed too quickly, even though they extended the meal by feeding each other berries and sipping their coffee as they compared notes on the evening before. All too soon they were heading back to Durkin and the demands of the day. When she'd agreed to serve Becky as maid of honor, she'd loved the idea of spending the whole day with her cousin on the most important day of her life. That, of course, was before Damian.

He pulled the car to the curb a block before her mother's house. He turned to Jessi and, without a word, leaned over and kissed her. His hands cradled her shoulders; his mouth was firm, warm and demanding. Jessi poured all her love and regret into that kiss, a silent goodbye she so didn't want to give.

The siren of an ambulance broke the moment. Again without speaking, Damian dropped the car into drive and covered the short distance to where Molly waited. He took Jessi's hand as they walked up to the door and squeezed it before he turned the handle for her to precede him in.

Her mother was full of questions about the reunion and everyone who'd been there. Jessi welcomed the coffee her mother handed her. They'd spent the night in bed but hadn't gotten much sleep. A hearty dose of caffeine was exactly what she needed. IV injections of pure black chicory coffee would be even better.

"So did you enjoy yourself last night or were you bored?" Molly directed the question to Damian.

"I loved every moment of it," he said. "I have Jessi to thank for that, of course."

"That's my girl. She'll give all she has."

Jessi bit her lip to hide the temptation to laugh. If her mother had any idea what her little girl had been doing, she doubted if praise would be coming her way. More like her mother's face flaming red and her fleeing the room as she pretended her precious baby would never do anything like that. Knowing Damian had booked a hotel room the previous night didn't mean she wanted to even think about the details.

The phone rang, the third time since they'd

gotten home. Her mother answered and was soon engrossed in another conversation about wedding details. Jessi found it hard to believe there was any stone left unturned in the quest for the perfect nuptials but her mother and aunt seemed to always be able to find one. She took advantage of her mother's preoccupation to head for hammock with her cell phone while Damian went upstairs to shower.

She called Destinee's phone, planning to leave a reminder about papers she'd need when she got back into the office. To her surprise, her assistant's chirpy hello greeted her instead of a recorded message.

"You did it," Destinee said.

"Did what?"

"Cleared your crystal. It was bright as sunshine when I left the office yesterday."

"You went to the office on a Saturday?"

"The fax machine tore up. The fix-it guy from the office supply store said he could come yesterday or come Monday. I thought you'd be happier if everything was working when you got back."

"Would this be the repairman you described as single and with a sexy butt?"

"Yes." Destinee gave a bright giggle. "He told me to call and ask for him personally if anything else happened to our equipment."

"You are not allowed to break things on purpose, remember."

Destinee giggled again which made Jessi think there might be more on the horizon for them than conversations about office equipment. She wondered how many crystal balls had been consulted in an attempt to make that happen.

"So how are things going?"

"The dress is every bit as hideous as I expected, the reunion activities were actually a blast and I'm headed for Becky's soon to get her dressed for the wedding and keep her calm."

"That's great. But what I mean is how are things going with you and you-know-who."

"My mom? I've loved spending time with her."

"Do not make me spell it out. I intend to get full disclosure when you get back but tell me you've been doing things that would make a porn star blush."

"I've enjoyed my time with Damian immensely. That's all you need to know. I actually just wanted to remind you that I need to review the contracts with those San Francisco firms as soon as I get to my desk. That's the only loose end I left hanging."

"Yes, ma'am, I'll take care of it. Now forget about me and this place and have fun. That's an order."

Her mother was still on the phone, or maybe back on it, when she came back into the house. Although trees shaded the hammock, Jessi still felt sticky from being out in the heat. After being assured that her mother had everything under control, she went up to see if Damian had left any hot water.

She found him in the guest room, wearing only boxers, with his suitcase open on top of the dresser. She settled on the bed to watch as his elegant clothing went back into the bag. A different dark suit than the one he'd worn the night before hung from the closet door leading her again to wonder how many suits he actually owned.

"You're packing already?"

He nodded. "I'm leaving on a red eye flight tonight."

"Oh." She'd assumed he would go the next day as she was. This really was almost the end. She couldn't leave the reception early and it sounded like he wouldn't

Page 209

be able to stay for the whole thing. So that's how this would end, with him slipping away like Cinderella from the ball.

She didn't bother with any of the usual follow-up to that kind of remark. He wasn't going to call. She didn't have to ask when she'd see him again because it wouldn't happen. She wondered if she'd get a thank you gift after she got home the same one she'd gotten those gifts before she'd left for Michigan. She hoped not. Flowers or candy would serve only to deepen the pain of his loss.

"What time do you have to be at your cousin's?" He paused in his packing to look at her.

Jessi glanced at the clock radio by the bed. "In an hour or so."

"Want to go for ice cream first?"

"Love to, but it's Sunday. The shop doesn't open until one."

"How about a walk?"

"Sure." She watched Damian pull on his clothes with graceful and economical movements, one more experience she'd never have again.

They talked about inconsequential things as they

strolled, hands linked. He asked about the floral clock at the park. She told the story of how the fire hall burned while the firefighters were at a blaze on the other side of town, which is why the new building was made of brick. They saw a few dogs and fewer people, reminding Jessi again of the huge difference between her small hometown and the city that never seemed to sleep.

Damian drove her to Becky's and dropped her off with a quick kiss goodbye. She stood outside the house, her dress bag draped over her arm, and watched him drive away. That was the last image she'd had of her father, driving down the street toward his office while she waited on the sidewalk for the bus. This, she decided, was the story of her life. The men she loved all went away.

"Hey, you lost?" Becky shouted through the screen door. "Come on in. The pizza's still hot."

The three bridesmaids were already there with curlers in their hair and perfect nails. Jessi glanced down at her own so-so fingernails. She'd put on a new coat of pale pink but lacked the length and perfect ovals of what she suspected were the artificial nails of the others. She hadn't even thought about a manicure. She hadn't even

Page 211

looked in the mirror to see if she needed her eyebrows waxed.

"Gloriana's coming in about an hour to start our hair."

Jessi seemed to be the only one surprised by Becky's announcement. She'd figured on hitting hers with the curling iron. It's not like anyone would notice thanks to the hair decoration she was being forced to wear. Then again, she'd managed somehow to forget that this was Becky's production and everything had to be perfect.

"You have wonderful hair," Gloriana gushed, running her fingers through Jessi's locks. "So thick and well nourished. I can do so much with it."

Jessi knew that was supposed to be compliment but after seeing the sprayed updos on the bridesmaids all she could do was hope that "wonderful hair" translated into "You'll still look normal." That hope was dashed when she was forced to produce the flower-loaded comb that would serve as the accent to her dress. A half-hour later she was staring at herself in the mirror praying that she could somehow duck out of every picture taken during the entire day. If she hadn't watched the whole process, she would have accused Gloriana of adding a hairpiece or maybe an entire wig to put such a wild riot of curls on her head. Granted, the hairdresser had offered her services free because of her friendship with Becky, but Jessi would have paid the airfare for her own stylist to fly in and leave looking, well, more like a human than a 1970s store mannequin.

"Oh, I can't wait until you guys are all dressed." Becky wiggled from what Jessi figured was excitement. Either that or she'd had way too much caffeine for a bride who was walking down the aisle in two hours.

As soon as she escaped from the temporary salon in her aunt's kitchen, Jessi found a quiet place outside and called Damian. Just hearing his voice was like an oasis of calm in the hectic preparations going on around her. Her head ached from a lack of sleep and the hairpins jabbed against her scalp. Her feet ached from standing and dancing all evening at the reunion. And her heart ached knowing she was stuck here when she wanted only to be with him.

"Having fun?" he asked.

"Sure." She made herself smile as she fibbed. "Becky and I used to play wedding with our dolls and I swear, every idea she had then she's using now."

Damian's laugh, as crisp as if he were sitting right beside her, lifted her spirits. She filed it in the treasure box of her memory, a jewel to comfort her when aloneness attacked her.

His laughter continued as she described her time at Gloriana's hands and she knew he meant it when he said he could hardly to see her again. He wanted a good look at her head.

"I just finished mowing the lawn for your mother," he said. "Give me time to take a shower and I can come steal you away."

"Becky will plow you down and hogtie you," she warned. "I promised her when I was twelve years old that I'd be her maid of honor and she'd be mine. You've only seen her good side. She has a streak of mean a mile wide."

That short conversation helped more than she expected. The time flew by as she dressed and then helped Becky get ready. The last thing she'd expected when she stepped into Becky's closet to get her wedding gown was how traditional it was. Granted, the skirt had layers of fluff and there were sequins galore added to the lace but it was pure white, full length and very much like the kind they're pretended their dolls were getting married in.

"Nervous?" she asked as she fluffed the skirt while they waited for the limo Tim had rented.

"Scared to death." Becky gave a nervous smile. "I love Tim so much and there's nothing I want more than to be married to him. This is a big step, though. Maybe I should have moved in with him when he asked me. At least I'd know already know if he hated my cooking or thought I had lousy taste in curtains."

"Don't." Jessi gave her cousin a loose hug. "You two are perfect for each other. I don't believe in the concept of soul mates but if I did, you and Tim would define it. He is one lucky man."

"And so is Damian. You do realize you're having a big wedding and I'm standing up with you, right?"

Oh, man. That was so something she didn't even want to think about.

"Don't change the subject," she scolded. "And trust me, men don't really care what you feed them as long as there's plenty of it and they don't notice curtains, either."

The honk that signaled the limo's arrival brought the noise and excitement in the house to a new level. The bridesmaids climbed in first. Jessi held her cousin's train as she settled in with care. She waved to her aunt and uncle who were heading for the church in their own car.

Settling back against the soft leather seat, she let the chatter swirl around her. Becky was beautiful today, with the glow that a bride ought to have. Jessi wondered if Tim was nervous or just impatient for them to arrive and the ceremony to begin. The latter, she decided. He was a study in self-confidence.

The limo slowed to make the turn into the church lot. The driver pulled to the back entrance; while Jessi helped Becky out of the car, the bridesmaids rushed in to make sure Tim wasn't anywhere around. It was bad luck, after all, for the groom to see the bride in her gown before she began her walk down the aisle.

"I can't believe I'm actually getting married," a giddy Becky said as they stepped into the small room set aside for the women.

"You've only been clipping pictures from bride

magazines since you were twelve," Jessi teased. "Remember when you made the dog marry the cat from next door?"

"You did not!" came from a bridesmaid as they all laughed.

"Oh, she did," Jessi affirmed. "Poor Buster wore a tissue paper veil despite the fact that he was a male and she shoved the neighbor's cat into one of her doll dresses. Luckily Mrs. Westfall was a good sport. She even took pictures of her Pookie getting hitched."

"Hey, I was like five," Becky protested. "We all do stuff like that when we're kids. Jessi ran around with aluminum foil bracelets pretending she was Wonder Woman."

By the time the photographer arrived to take photos of their final preparations, the mood was perfect for relaxed and sometimes silly pictures. Even Becky's mother laughed rather than cried as she hugged her daughter before turning her over to her father to be walked to the altar.

When it came Jessi's turn to precede the bride, she took a deep breath and concentrated on walking the right speed to keep the procession timed just as Becky wanted it. Seeing Damian near the front settled her; his proud smile served as reassurance that yes, she would do fine.

Jessi accepted Becky's flowers as she was supposed to and remembered to untie the groom's ring from the pillow carried by the ring bearer before the minister asked for it. She handed the bridal bouquet back after the ceremony-ending kiss that brought loud applause from the assembled guests. And somehow, through it all, she forgot that she was wearing a gaudy dress with a flower spray in her artificial curls.

The photos after the ceremony took an eternity. Jessi's feet began to cramp in the new shoes and her face ached from the continual smiles the photographer demanded. Relief filled here when the attendants were released so the happy couple and their parents could pose for even more scrapbook pictures.

"Congratulations," Damian greeted her as she met him at the back of the sanctuary. "It looks like you're a free woman. Your mother sent an outfit along in case you want to change before the reception."

Jessi glanced down at her gown. "You don't want to be seen with me in this adorable frock?"

"Darling, I'd be proud to be seen with you even if you were wearing a clown suit and red nose."

"Probably because then I could get you free tickets for the circus."

Laughing, Damian led her outside to wait for the couple to exit the church. Jessi waved at her mother, who was standing in the midst of a group of relatives, and accepted the bubble bottle handed to her by one of the younger cousins. Damian stepped behind her, his hands on her waist, as she took her place with the line of bridesmaids. When the church doors open and Becky and Tim stepped out hand in hand, she lifted the tiny plastic stick to her lips and blew. Her bubbles joined the others to float around the couple as they ran to the limo.

"So are you two next?" The casual question came from a friend of her mother's, reminding Jessi how fast news spread in a small town.

"We haven't even started to make plans," Damian answered for her. "She insists on a long engagement which makes sense with our crazy schedules. Besides, it takes a lot to buy a rose-covered cottage these days so I'm saving like crazy."

"Oh, you." He received a light swat on the arm

from the middle-aged woman. "You just better not elope. Molly would have both your hides."

The crowd began to disperse. People headed toward their cars and pick-ups for the drive to the reception hall. Jessi saw her name on a place card at the long table for the wedding party and sighed. She wanted only to be with Damian but duty called. Although, she realized, maybe it was better this way. Maybe a gradual separation wouldn't be as painful when he had to leave.

And maybe pigs would fly through the hall at any second.

****

"Ladies and gentlemen, please make way for Mr. and Mrs. Timothy and Rebecca Canfield!"

The DJ's voice carried through the hall to be replaced by cheers and applause as the newlyweds made their entrance. A wave of aahs came when Tim swept Becky into his arms and carried her in. The look of adoration on his face was exquisite; Jessi wished she had a camera. But Becky's squeal of "I'm slipping" broke the moment and brought a light-hearted feeling to the room.

The meal was delicious, interrupted by the clink

of spoons on glasses and demands for the couple to kiss. Jessi attempted conversation with the best man, who was seated next to her, but her focus was on Damian. Sitting with her mother and two couples who looked very familiar, he seemed to be having a good time. She smiled when he noticed her and winked. The toasts were about to start and then, at long last, the music would begin.

Her toast was short and sincere unlike the one given by Tim's brother which was risqué enough to bring an objection from his mother. A few more toasts, a little more spoon clinking and demands for kisses, and the bride and groom took the floor for their special dance. Jessi suspected they'd been practicing because she'd always thought that Tim had two left feet. Now, though, he led Becky across the floor in a waltz worthy of a dance contest show.

Damian waited with an outstretched hand when the announcement came for others to join the couple. Jessi stepped into his arms and looked up into his face. His features were somber which made the moment even more bittersweet.

"Mind if I cut in?" Ryan tapped Damian on the

shoulder. Jessi glanced over to where Heather sat looking miserable. Being pregnant and partying two nights in a row was probably not a good combination. She was glad Damian joined her friend as she and Ryan danced.

"He's great, you know," Ryan said.

"Oh, I know."

"Please don't let your ambition kill this for you. Making a success of your company is great but there's a lot to be said for family life."

Jessi studied him. "Back in high school you wanted to be a forest ranger. Are you ever sorry you stayed here instead?"

He shook his head. "I was too young to realize what is really important. Waking up with my beautiful wife every day and tucking the kids into bed at night is all I need."

Although she walked off the floor intending to join Damian, her progress was interrupted by one person after another, from her mother's friends to old school acquaintances. Precious moments slipped away as she answered questions and exchanged pleasantries. A tiny fission of panic ran through her. What if Damian left before she could get to him? What if she didn't get to say goodbye?

She was saved when he showed up with a glass of wine and a smile of apology for the woman he stole her from. She sipped the sweet liquid and sighed. Tranquil. She needed to stay tranquil. She would not allow her last memory of their time together to be of her freaking out.

"Care to dance?" He took her half-empty glass without waiting for an answer and set it on the tray on a table behind them. Grasping her hand, he led her to a secluded corner of the dance floor reached by only dim light. A potted palm partially blocked them from the others and allowed a bit of privacy. Jessi melted against him, wrapping her arms around his neck so their bodies were tight.

She had no idea what music played. She knew only that it was slow; they swayed, their feet barely moving. She concentrated on capturing everything about him, from the scent of soap and aftershave that was uniquely his to the curve of muscle in his arms around her. She stared into his eyes, memorizing the tiny flecks of green and gold in their dark depths.

"Don't leave me."

She wasn't too proud to beg.

"I have no choice." Those wonderful eyes mirrored the regret deep in her soul.

"Then I'll go with you."

"I can't let you. Too many people depend on you."

"I don't care. Please stay. Please."

Damned tears welled again. For a woman who never cried, she seemed to do nothing else since she got back to Durkin. But she couldn't lose him. Not again. She loved Daelfin too much.

Damian. She was being held by Damian.

"I can't." His voice was rough. "I've broken your heart often enough. If I go now, this time it will heal."

Before she could ask for an explanation, the music changed into something modern and clanging. As if it were a signal, Damian bent his head and kissed her. A powerful sense of loss overwhelmed her and she knew it was time. Whatever had sent him to her was calling him back.

When he stepped away, she swallowed back

another plea for him to stay. The inevitable couldn't be changed. Destiny was inflexible.

"I'll always love you," she murmured.

"You always have," he whispered, sliding his fingers down her cheek before turning and walking away. Jessi wrapped her arms around herself, her heart breaking as she watched him disappear.

"Are you all right, dear?"

She turned at her mother's words.

"No." Her voice broke. "I may never be okay again."

Molly patted her arm. "It's not as if you'll never see him again. I'm not a believer in long-distance relationships but yours certainly seems to work."

Since there was nothing she could stay to that, Jessi remained quiet. Forcing a smile, she walked back to the table where Heather waited. She took the chair next to her and concentrated on being the perfect wedding guest, thrilled at her cousin's obvious joy even though she'd never be happy again.

Riding home, Jessi hoped her mother would take her silence for exhaustion. Tomorrow she'd sit at the table and rehash the wedding and everything that followed. Tonight she wanted to hug those last moments to her, to treasure them before they began to fade. And they would.

Pulling up and not seeing the rental car was hard. Walking upstairs to her room was far more difficult knowing that the room across the hall was impersonal once again. She didn't walk into see if she could catch a left behind scent or feel him there. He was gone. Tormenting herself couldn't change that.

She unzipped the dress and let it drop onto the floor. Pulling the flowers from her hair, she tossed them on top of the ridiculous gown and walked to the bathroom. Hot water melted the hairspray and a good shampooing and dose of conditioner made her feel more like herself. She dried off, pulled on her nightgown and went to bed, feeling more alone than she ever had before.

Chapter Eleven

"Wake, my sweetness." Daelfin's whisper and soft shake woke her from the light sleep that had overtaken her. "You must return to your bed before we are discovered."

She uttered a small mew of protest. The bed was warm, his body comforting. Now that she had experienced what the maids whispered about behind their hands, she wanted to do it again. And again.

"You must go." Daelfin became more insistent. "I will confess to your father so you may remain blameless. I will tell him I drank too much and seduced you, mistaking you for a loose woman."

"No." The denial burst from her in fury. "I will not lie; neither shall you. You are my beloved."

"Oh, my innocent." Daelfin curled his hand around her chin. "Your father will see only that you have been defiled. You will be sent away to hide his shame. All he has will weaken and fall because of what we have done. Do not let such a thing happen, I beg of you."

Sorrow walked with her as she obeyed. They

would never be together again. She knew that deep within her soul. Yet his words were clear in her memory.

"I watched you die yet here you are in my embrace."

A flicker of hope grew inside her as she washed herself with the cold water from the ewer and climbed into her bed. In the midst of their lovemaking, he had called her by another name. Called her Fiona.

She had heard of those who lived before and whose goodness was rewarded by another turn on earth. Had she been among them? Had he?

When the sun finally rose after her fitful sleep, she hiked across the hall to where Daelfin slept. The bed was empty, as neatly made as if it had never been used. He was gone, although a hint of his scent remained. She inhaled deeply, wanting to imprint it upon her very soul.

Remarkably, the chief guard seemed not to notice a difference when she sought him to inquire about their visitor. Word had come from her father; the messenger had gone to meet him.

Hope flared. Surely they would return together. She would watch. If her father held him in regard, perhaps a union could be arranged.

The moon rose and set twice before a rider arrived to announce that preparations should begin. Isobel hurried to the kitchen to consult with the cook. Her father's arrival should be celebrated with a feast. The skirmishes along the border lands grew increasingly fierce, the danger ever greater.

The small procession came in a cloud of dust. Isobel stood upon the high stones to watch the riders as they passed through the gate. Her father rode at the head upon the tall black steed who shared the battles with him. His soldiers rode behind, two by two, their weariness showed in the slump of their bodies.

Isobel clasped her hands to her breast, slumping against the wall when they came near enough to see their faces. He was not with them. Daelfin had been left behind.

Mayhap he was dead.

She shoved the macabre thought away and rushed down the steps to greet her father with an embrace despite his odor and dirty garments. Gratitude rushed through her at his safe return. The burden of running the keep was heavy and one she would happily give to him again.

Page 229

*"You look well." Her father smiled, an upturned
line among the dust he wore.*

"So shall you when that filth is gone."

*With a chuckle, he patted her hair and suggested
that she check upon the heating water. Isobel ran to do
as he requested, partly in obedience but also to keep
from blurting out the question burning within her. Had
Daelfin reached him or did he lie lifeless?*

Jessi woke in a tangle of sheets and a sheen of
sweat. Blinking to clear the sleep from her eyes, she
managed to undo her trappings and get up. The sweet
life she'd had here in Durkin was over. The chiming of
her cell phone alarm was her first reminder. The second
was the lack of breakfast aromas in the house. She was
leaving today and her mother had suggested they have
breakfast on the way to the airport.

She took a quick, refreshing shower and dressed
in dark slacks and a white sleeveless shirt. It didn't take
long to pack, and she remembered to keep out a jacket.
Airports and planes were always cold.

"Oh, honey, I hate to see you go." Molly greeted
her from the downstairs foyer.

"And I hate to leave. A day of doing nothing right here with you would be wonderful."

"But you have a plane ticket and a business to run." She glanced at the clock above the sink. "We better leave now if we're having breakfast."

They stopped at a local diner known for its French toast and veggie omelets. Jessi ordered one, her mother the other, so that they could each have a little of both. Breaking her low-carb rule for the millionth time since she got to Durkin, she slathered butter and poured maple syrup over the egg-covered bread and enjoyed every bite. It was probably a good thing she'd moved away or she'd be as big as the prize-winning cow at the county fair.

The service was good and the food had come promptly from the kitchen, leaving them time to linger over coffee during this last meal together. Jessi would have loved to talk about anything her Mom chose except what she brought up.

"Damian is wonderful," she said. "You're so lucky to have met him. I knew when I met your father that he was the only one for me and I can tell you feel that way about Damian. And he obviously adores you."

Page 231

Jessi waited for her mother to add the inevitable remark about it being time for her to get married and produce grandchildren. She was surprised at her mother's next words.

"I don't know what the future holds for the two of you but I want you to promise me one thing. Don't let life pass you by. Money and success are wonderful things but what really matters are the things you can't see or sell."

Jessi wasn't sure whether Mom was giving a general admonition or speaking from her own experience. No matter. The advice was good. Much as she hated to admit it, Destinee was right. She did need to get out more. She should accept some of the offers for dinner. Her work was no substitute for a relationship even if marriage wasn't in the cards.

Saying goodbye outside the security checkpoint was harder than she expected. Harder than it had ever been before. These few days in Durkin had changed her. Seeing it through Damian's eyes had shown her nuances of life in her hometown that she might never have noticed without him.

After one final hug, Jessi waved goodbye to her

mother, took off her shoes and started through the inspection process. She found a chair near her gate and picked up a discarded newspaper. She suddenly realized she hadn't read a paper or even watched the TV news since she left home. Time to catch up with the real world.

Her flight was smooth, the landing uneventful. She snagged a cab within minutes of walking outside the terminal and traffic was light on the ride to her place. Her waiting apartment was quiet and cool. She'd set the air conditioning timer to kick on an hour before her flight landed.

The sterility she'd noticed in the condo before she left still bothered her. The house in Durkin was full of colors, from the yellow walls of the kitchen to the bright pillows on the sofa. Even the front door was painted red because her mother thought the wide siding and gray porch floor were drab.

Four years. That's how long she'd lived in this place yet her personality didn't show. Her office was more reflective of who she was and she had been careful to keep it looking all business. She snapped on the television for background noise and turned on her laptop. Maybe she'd check out one of those "fabulous discount" sites just to see what they offered.

She'd put a serious dent in her wallet by the time she was done. Within the next week or two, she would be the proud owner of red enamel cookware, a set of blue throw rugs for the living room, a line green bedspread and a set of frog figurines she planned to put atop the entertainment center. Tomorrow she'd stop at that little art gallery near her office and look for prints that caught her fancy.

She stayed up later than she'd planned and fell quickly into a sleep so deep that if she dreamed, she didn't remember. She woke before the alarm, did her routine of stretching exercises and wrote out a grocery list before she left for the office.

"Morning, boss lady." Destinee met her with a cup of tea. Jessi sniffed it with suspicion; given the events of the last week, she was wary of hallucinogenics. It carried the scent of raspberry so she decided to give it a chance.

"Did you find the files I need?" Jessi crossed the room. She intended to hide behind her desk before the cross-examination could begin.

She should have known better.

"They're right here." Destinee held them up and wiggled the manila folders at her. "We have things to talk about first."

"No, we don't." Jessi stretched out her arm and waited for her assistant to hand over the paperwork. Tipping her head, she adopted her best iron lady stare. When she was ready, she'd share a little of her escape to Michigan. But only a little.

"Don't make me call your mother!" Destinee shouted after her, the last word cut off by the slamming of Jessi's office door.

Pink phone call notes were neatly stacked by her phone. As always, Destinee had sorted them by date and importance of call. Jessi sighed. It was amazing how fast she could get behind in just a few days. She logged onto her e-mail with trepidation. Nearly four hundred messages. Yeah, a fair share were obvious spam but she still had to look through the others.

The day went fast as she whittled down the callbacks and messages. Destinee brought her a vegetarian, no-fat sub when she returned from lunch which Jessi wolfed down. She thought ruefully that all the fiber, vegetables and good stuff would be a huge shock to her system.

Acknowledging Destinee's goodbye with a wave, she opened the first of the folders she'd avoided all day. There were six of them; each represented a different city but the same familiar two to three days of training. She was looking at a month's worth of work which was great for the bottom line. But profit and loss sheets had lost their appeal.

She tucked the locket that hung beneath the fabric of her top. As soon as things slowed down she was going to one of those do-it-yourself photo places and print off a picture of Damian to put inside. The man might be gone but she still intended to keep him close to her heart.

The ring of her cell phone made her jump. The last person she expected it to be was Ryan. The last news she wanted to hear was that Heather had been hospitalized.

"Why?" she demanded. "When?"

"About two hours ago. Her blood pressure's way up and the doctor said the baby's in stress."

"Do you need me to come back and help with the

kids?"

"No, no. The moms plan to take turns staying with them so I can be at the hospital. She wanted to make sure you knew, that's all, so you don't think she's blowing off her offer to download the reunion videos and send them to you."

"Oh, my gosh, Ryan, that's the last thing she should worry about now."

She pressed for more details on what the doctors had said but was only slightly reassured when she said goodbye. Heather had been her absolute best friend for so many years. Over the last few days, that connection had come back. Or so Jessi had thought. It pained her that Heather's purpose in having Ryan call wasn't to let her know of the crisis but because of a stupid video.

She closed her eyes and leaned back in her chair. She'd known her success would come with a price; she hadn't realized how high it could be.

Jessi stopped at the all night megastore on her way home. Downloading a week's worth of photos on a CD didn't take long but it seemed to take forever for the dozen or so she intended to frame to print. Fishing them out of the plastic tray at last, she smiled at one of her being silly with Heather. She flipped through to make sure she had them all and swallowed hard at the one of Damian and her at Becky's wedding. God, they looked happy. It seemed impossible that only an hour or so later, he was gone. Forever.

She stuck the CD back into the machine and found that shot again. After a couple of tries she managed to crop herself out and the resulting head shot of Damian to fit in the locket. She'd talked herself out of it but that was before she saw his beloved face on that 4x6.

An impulse had her reaching for an inexpensive bouquet of bright flowers at the checkout. Back at her condo, she found a vase under the sink and arranged them. She nodded in satisfaction at the way they looked on the credenza in the living room.

She unwrapped the frames she'd bought during her impromptu shopping trip. A sitcom played in the background as she trimmed the photos to fit the mats and frames she'd picked up. By rearranging books and pieces of crystal on the dining room shelves she managed to create a cozy piece of Durkin back here in

Atlanta.

Jessi picked up the one framed picture she intended to keep beside her bed. A smile curved across her face as she studied her mother's face. They didn't look alike. Jessi favored her father with her oval face and dark hair. In personality though, she was so like Mom. She promised herself to stay trusting and open like her mother, to roll with the punches life threw at her no matter how hard they hit.

"You're getting maudlin," she scolded herself. The roller coaster of emotions her sojourn in Michigan had inflicted was definitely getting the best of her. Appreciate the past and anticipate the future. Her father had often offered that as advice when she ran to him with some regret.

Her thoughts as she dropped off to sleep that night were on Heather and Becky. They were both taking bold new steps. Yeah, Heather had other children but those pregnancies had been textbook perfect. She couldn't imagine the thoughts running through her head as she lay in a hospital bed.

Becky should already be in San Francisco. Tim had indulged her lifelong dream to see the city by surprising her with a five-day honeymoon before he left. Jessi was sure that her e-mail inbox would hold photos from California the next day. She hoped there was a really good one of the newlyweds that she could add to her collection.

Isobel clutched her stomach and ran out into the garden as her breakfast prepared to come up. The lamb cook served last night had a delicious taste yet it seemed not to agree with her. Lately many things did not seem to set well. Seeking privacy behind a tree, she bent over and retched praying none overheard. Anne's voice startled her.

"Does your father know?"

"Know what?" Isobel asked her maid, perplexed.

"That you are with child."

"I am not! Twas only last night's meal."

Anne shook her head slowly. "There are twelve children in my family. I've seen my mother in the same condition many times."

Isobel's eyes widened and she sought the solid bench nearby. Twice. She had lain with Daelfin only twice and both times the same night. Others spent night after night with men and yet their bellies stayed flat. Dread and fear warred with excitement within her. Her subtle inquiries had brought her no information about her beloved. Her heart told her he no longer lived. Yet a piece of him still survived, cradled within her body.

"Tell him now and he will find you a husband." Anne grasped her hands and spoke in an urgent voice. "It must be done now before your shame can be seen. Men are gullible. Your husband will believe that it is his, eager to enter the world when it comes a bit early."

"I cannot." Isobel was repulsed by the very idea of lying with another man, of his hands mauling her as he forced himself upon her. She would die first.

"Then tell him and let him send you away. Others will believe that you travel to visit distant family and once the child is born and given to a suitable family, you can return with no one the wiser."

Give his child up? Isobel folded her hands across her belly as if to protect the new life she carried. She would not be forced to such an action.

"You have no other choices," Anne urged. "Marry or be hidden away. To do else is impossible if

Page 241

your father is to remain in power."

The day dragged as she waited for the right time to approach her father. As she built her courage to speak to him and confess her sin. Anne's words, like sharp barbs, had poked her conscience ever since that moment in the garden. He was a good man, a good lord to his people, and she must throw herself upon his mercy.

The blare of a fire engine brought her abruptly awake. The siren sounded close; she jumped out of bed and ran to the window. The long red ladder truck continued past her complex to turn at the corner. Relieved but definitely not able to go back to sleep now, she shut off the alarm and went to the kitchen to start the coffee dripping. Remnants of the dream stayed with her as she stepped into the shower. Pregnant. Poor girl. One night was all it took. Of course, back then there were no ninety-nine percent effective condoms, IUDs or birth control pills. She was quite grateful that Damian had arrived in Michigan with a supply of the first. Although she was pretty sure she couldn't have the baby of a being that didn't exist.

Whoa, it was way too early in the day for metaphysical thoughts. She began to mentally review her schedule for the day. A few workshop evaluations to review, a meeting with the accountant and an after-hours business social at the bank down the street. She'd only been back one day and she was back in the groove.

"Morning, boss lady." Destinee took one last deep breath of the sage and settled at her desk. "I just got a call from some dude planning a conference for plumbers or something like that. Anyway he wanted to know if you'd be available for a half-day presentation."

"For plumbers?" Jessi had trouble envisioning their need for table etiquette.

"Maybe it was water system administrators. Something like that."

"Give me the number and I'll call him back."

The group turned out to be environmental engineers and the request was for training on conference calls and webinars. Jessi was pleased with the conversation after she hung up. She was confident enough to pencil the January date in her desk planner.

Her meeting with the accountant took longer than she'd expected. As she settled back in at her desk she realized she'd missed lunch and wasn't even hungry. That was fine with her after everything she'd eaten in Durkin.

Everything she and Damian had eaten. Ice cream, picnic foods, that marvelous lemon meringue pie – they'd turned dining into an art while they were together. And, she realized, she hadn't been the least bit self-conscious eating with him.

****

Molly caught the phone on the first ring and recognized the number immediately.

"Hello honey," she said.

"Wrong honey," Destinee replied. "Jessi's out of town until tomorrow night so I thought I'd call for an update."

Molly sighed. "Oh, I wish I had one. Our calls have been short and just so matter of fact. Whenever I ask about Damian, she says he's fine and changes the subject. Do you know more than me?"

"I know she's working too hard and losing weight. Lately she's walked into the office right after me and I sneaked onto her computer to see when she quit last night. She closed the last text file at almost nine p.m."

"No Damian?"

"No." The word came from Destinee on a sigh. "She won't talk about him either. Her aura has been violently blue, which is not a good sign, and I don't think she's sleeping well. I'm thinking depression."

Molly let Destinee's diagnosis sink in. She knew her daughter was worried about her friend Heather and Becky would soon be a left-at-home bride as well. Jessi was such a caring person that she carried other people's worries as her own. But depression was such a serious thing.

"Maybe she's just blue."

"Or lovesick," Destinee suggested. "If he's out of her life that could explain everything."

"Oh, he wouldn't leave her. Damian adores Jessi."

Talking with Destinee was so easy and comforting. Molly found herself pouring out all the little things that worried her from her daughter's reluctance to talk about their future plans to her own fear that she would never have grandchildren. She'd been looking forward to that experience for Jessi's whole life.

Still she was a little disappointed when the conversation ended. Destinee had been vague which made her believe there was more to her daughter's romance than met the eye. Well, she had a computer and plenty of time. If there were secrets to ferret out, she'd find them.

By the time she gave up her eyes burned and her carpal tunnel problems had flared up again. She found a few but none of them were him. Some of the pictures weren't very good but the quality was still high enough that she knew that.

She sat down with her grocery pad and a pen that had come from the hospital open house. Old-fashioned sleuthing might be what was needed. She drew a line down the center of the page. On one side she jotted clues from her conversations with Damian and on the other side she listed things Jessi had said.

She started with the story of their meeting. Damian had said they'd met when she accidentally picked up his order. Molly was pretty sure her daughter usually had food delivered or ate something Destinee brought when she went for her own lunch.

She listed separate rooms on both sides. Despite

her little lecture she had anticipated one or the other sneaking across the hall. If they were as crazy about each other as they seemed, they'd be used to sleeping together and find a way to do it even in her house.

Then there was Jessi's new affection for bowling. The one area of her father's life she dropped out of after she hit high school was that sport. She didn't even want to go along to play the video games and eat a hot dog while he was at the lanes. Yet she seemed excited to go along with Damian.

Fifteen minutes passed while she concentrated on making her list. Once she was done, she grabbed her purse and keys and headed for her sister's house. There was plenty of time for them to brainstorm with Becky on her honeymoon.

****

Thank heavens for work. That was the only thing keeping Jessi sane. The dream came almost every night now. She retained only snatches that didn't seem to connect yet the emotions it evoked stayed with her. The loss and despair she felt when she woke mirrored her waking feelings whenever she thought about Damian. She appreciated the bitter irony of finally falling in love

Page 247

only to realize he was the one man she could never have.

One bright spot was Heather's improved health. Jessi had been keeping in regular contact and was thrilled that although this baby might come early, it wouldn't be a fragile preemie. Experiencing the heartache of losing someone she loved had given her a greater empathy for others. She simply couldn't imagine how it would feel to lose a child.

"Call for you on two!" Destinee shouted from her desk. Jessi picked up the receiver and answered with her usual professional greeting.

Her aunt was on the line.

"Your mother didn't want you to worry but she wound up in the emergency room last night," she said. "The doctor thinks it may be her heart so she's scheduled for tests over the next couple of days. I figured you'd want to know."

An icy fear formed around Jessi's heart. She couldn't lose her mother. Not now. Not until Molly was an old, old lady decades from now.

"I'll be there tonight."

"Honey, wait till the weekend. She's feeling okay this morning. I insisted she stay with me just in case she gets to feeling bad again. If anything turns up, I'll let you know as soon as I do. Okay?"

No, that was not okay. Mom had patched up her skinned knees and hurt feelings, fed her chicken soup when she had the measles and stayed up all night when she spiked a fever. Still, she of all people knew how stubborn her mother could be. If Jessi showed up in a panic she might just have another heart episode.

"Okay," she finally agreed. "I'll catch an afternoon flight on Friday."

They chatted for a few minutes about the practical details, whether Jessi should rent a car or have someone pick her up. Jessi jotted down the number of the cardiologist's office and double-checked the hospital's. Her heart was heavy as she hung up the phone.

"What's wrong?" Destinee appeared in the doorway.

"Mom. She had to go to the ER last night and they think it might be a heart problem."

"No wonder you have a gray cloud around you. I'll be right back."

The tiny charm Destinee brought in looked like a

tangled knot but she insisted it was a talisman for healing and spiritual calming. Rather than protest as she usually did, Jessi took the silver charm and the pink crystal Destinee handed her and put them in her pocket. Carrying them on her person might not help a thing but it wasn't going to hurt either. And she knew that Destinee, who felt close to Molly, needed someone to feel like she was supporting them both.

Daily updates came via her aunt's phone calls. Jessi gained a little confidence when she realized how serious everyone was taking her mother's problem. Not only had she had tests Jessi knew were common but she'd had some that were totally foreign.

The last call on Thursday before Jessi left the office was another update. Mom had failed her heart stress test so a heart cath was set for the following afternoon. Jessi caught Destinee before she got out the door and told her to cancel everything for the next day. It was time to go back to Michigan.

By the time Jessi landed in Detroit, the only vehicles left at her regular rental company were mini-vans and the tiniest compact car she'd ever seen. She hit the highway for home in a pure white, eight-passenger soccer mommy van with tinted windows and every option possible. She cursed when it started to sprinkle. This thing had to have wipers but damned if she could find them. She pulled off and started peering at the buttons on the steering column. She finally got the right one just as the light rain stopped.

That was the final straw. She sat in the mini-van with the hazard signal flashing and bawled like a two-year-old. She cried because her mother was sick, cried because the door to a tantalizing life of love and family had slammed shut, cried because she was thirty-two years old with a life some people envied yet she was absolutely miserable. By the time her tears ran out, it was raining again. She pulled onto the road and stopped at the first place offering coffee she could find.

Her makeup disappeared as she splashed cold water on her tear-stained face and patted it dry with toilet paper. She wasn't about to stick her head in front of the high-powered air dryer. When she decided she was presentable, she fixed herself a cup of half regular and half vanilla cappuccino, grabbed a chocolate granola bar and a bag of chips and went to the counter to pay. She stopped dead in her tracks when a tall, dark-haired man crossed her line of vision. Clutching her choices, she checked the aisle until she saw him again. Her heart caught. Oh dear heavens, could it really be him?

Crushing disappointment filled her when the man turned and she could plainly see it wasn't Damian. Stupid idea anyway, that coming to Michigan might trigger his return. He'd been a temporary hunk of protoplasm created for a specific period of time. Damian St. Clair did not exist except in her memories.

The combination of coffee and chocolate took care of the incipient headache her crying jag had caused. She crunched the chips, enjoying the verboten salt and carbs. Turning to food instead of booze in times of crisis had to be the better choice. At least she was safe behind the wheel with chip dust on her fingers.

Jessi expected the house to be dark when she pulled up at her aunt's; it was nearly midnight, after all. Instead she saw the figures of two women on the metal porch glider. Her secret was out.

"Hello, sweetheart." Molly came down the steps to hug her before Jessi could make it onto the porch. "I know I said you weren't to know but I'm so glad you're here."

While her aunt disappeared into the house to get the pitcher of iced tea and an empty glass for Jessi, she listened as her mother told the story and unloaded her fears. This was a side of Mom that Jessi hadn't seen before. Molly exuded confidence and an unshakeable sense that everything would be all right. Yet she was talking about how she wasn't ready to die yet.

For the first time in maybe her whole life, Jessi was at a loss for words. She could explain a formal dinner setting and introduce her mother to the proper way to greet Japanese business associates but she couldn't find the right thing to say to allay Mom's stark fears. Maybe that was because her own fear was growing.

Finally she poured out what was in her heart.

"You're all I have," she admitted. "All my life you've been my rock, encouraging me no matter now crazy my ideas sounded. I'm completely lost right now. I have no idea what to do."

"Pray." Her aunt offered the suggestion as she set a tray on a low table. "I've already got everyone else in town doing that."

****

Jessi was grateful for her aunt and her rock-hard faith as they sat in the waiting room the next afternoon. No way could she have survived this alone. And the quiet certainty that everything would be all right exuded by her aunt helped settle Jessi's nerves. The flutters of fear returned when her name was called to go to the small consult room where the cardiologist joined them. The man was straight-forward. Her mother had a problem with her heart but dietary changes, medicine and keeping an eye on things should keep her around for a long time yet.

Naturally her mother insisted on celebrating the news with a restaurant meal since they left the hospital right at dinner time.

"Consider this the last supper of the condemned," she remarked as she scanned the menu. "Tomorrow's soon enough to start with oatmeal and salads."

Jessi let it slide. If her mother wanted a baked potato topped with real butter and sour cream with her steak, that was okay. So was the cherry cheesecake she ordered for dessert. She had no doubt but what her mother would throw herself into her new lifestyle with the enthusiasm she had for every project.

While her mother napped the next morning, Jessi made a trip to the supermarket. By the time Molly woke her refrigerator was filled with low-fat milk, chicken breasts and cholesterol-cutting fake butter. Jessi held her breath with the first opening of the refrigerator door but her mother seemed to accept the changes well. She even praised the grilled chicken salads Jessi made for lunch and only complained a little about the low-fat ranch dressing.

"Remember today you rest." Jessi tapped the dismissal orders on the front of the refrigerator. "I picked up a movie for this afternoon and tonight I thought we'd have something light like egg white veggie omelets and fruit."

The argument she expected never came. Her mother was quite agreeable to all Jessi's plans. Jessi ran the vacuum, cleaned out the cupboards and did every other household task she figured her mother should avoid until the tiny incision healed. Mom was putting on a good face but her failure to protest revealed how this episode had scared her.

She slept on the living room couch Saturday

night, using the excuse that she wanted to be close to her mother's downstairs bedroom in case she was needed. In reality she wasn't ready to occupy her old room again. Not without Damian across the hall.

"You're too thin." Molly brushed sugar-free jam on her toast the next morning. "A few French fries wouldn't hurt you."

"It could in twenty years."

"Point taken. The doctor said these things can be hereditary. You don't want to be poked and prodded like I've been the last few days."

"He also said you can live to be a hundred provided you do what you're told."

Molly rolled her eyes. "Eating tofu and bean sprouts."

"Eating real food. I pulled some recipes off the Internet for you."

"Okay, you win. I'll do as I'm told if you promise to gain five pounds."

Jessi laughed. Her mother was definitely on the mend.

Chapter Thirteen

Sitting on the plastic seat waiting for the next leg of her flight home, Jessi realized again how much she hated airports. Everything seemed the same no matter where she was from the restaurants to the recycled air. Time fluctuated too. If she had a long layover, time dragged. But if she was rushing to catch a plane, it absolutely flew.

Right now the minutes were crawling. She had already read two of the newspapers left behind by other passengers and done the crossword puzzles. Sighing, she opened her tablet and pulled up a book she'd been meaning to read since spring. When the call to board came, she was pleased at how few were on the flight. She intended to sleep until the wheels touched down again.

Her condo door was a welcome sight. She unlocked it, stepped in and dropped her suitcase. The place was far more welcoming that it had been a few months ago. The air was scented with the fresh flowers she replaced once a week and bright pillows and throw rugs added color. She was gradually making it a home.

Although she was starving and wanted a shower, Jessi kept her promise and called her mother to let her know she made it home okay. She was relieved her mother sounded more like her regular self with an upbeat tone back in her voice. She made a pledge to get back to Durkin more often and to strengthen her relationship with her entire extended family. It had taken her three decades but she finally realized there were more important things in than prestige and money.

"Evangaline, I'd like you to meet my newest bookkeeper, Devon Fairchild."

Eva smiled at the man who stood at her father's left. He was tall with dark hair that reflected the sunlight and a body which complemented the suit he wore. His eyes were his most fascinating feature with gold and green flecks in their dark depths.

"I am most pleased to meet you," Devon said with a deep bow.

"As am I," she replied with an answering nod. She studied the stranger as her father finished giving instructions. She knew they had never met as her trips into Boston were few yet he seemed familiar. His stance,

the tip of his head as he listened, the scar upon his face...

Awareness dawned. She dreamed of him. Every few months the same scene came to her in her sleep. She was within castle walls, waiting for her father's return, when a messenger arrives. The hooded cloak he wore kept his features mostly covered. Still his eyes were unusual and unforgettable.

"Eva, did you hear me?"

Heat rose in her cheeks. Her father had spoken to her and she had not heard. Her concentration had been on the bookkeeper who was smiling at her as if he knew.

"I'm sorry, Father. I fear I was preoccupied."

"I have asked Mr. Fairchild to join us for lunch if you do not mind."

"Oh, certainly, please do."

Her father offered her a smile of approval. She had served as hostess for her father since her mother's death in a buggy accident when she was only fourteen. Perfect manners were important to him and what mattered to Father was of utmost concern to her as well.

Page 259

Jessi woke with a start, her heart racing. The dream had changed. Damian was still there but nothing else was right.

"I'm going flipping crazy," she muttered aloud. Her high school English teacher had encouraged her to pursue creative writing but Jessi didn't she had enough imagination for that. Apparently she was wrong.

She glanced at the bedside clock. Her wake-up was set for a half-hour later. If she tried to go to sleep now, she would drop off just as it started to ring. If she reset it for a little later, she'd miss a conference call set for nine. Sighing, she shut off the alarm and decided to pick up her morning coffee on the way to work instead of taking it with her. A double espresso was what she needed to jolt her into the right frame of mind.

She stepped into the shower and realized as she got out that, naturally, it had begun to rain. This day was doomed; she might as well throw in the towel now. Nothing good could possibly happen.

She logged onto her e-mail wondering if she could wait out the shower. A message from Heather assured her that all was well on the baby front. That was a piece of good news which might help offset the crap she was attracting today.

The rain had lessened but not disappeared by the time she walked out the door. She popped open her umbrella and rushed out into the parking lot. By the time she reached the office, her hair was in wild curls and her feet were damp from being forced to walk through parking lot puddles. Sighing, she calmed her hair was best she could and sat down in front of the camera on her computer. Her dream life was so much easier than her real one these days.

Tied up with the call, she didn't hear Destinee leave for lunch. Buried in planning how to do back-to-back workshops in LA one day and Maine the next day, she didn't hear her return. Her answer when Destinee asked if she'd had eaten was an absent-minded "I'm not hungry." And when a club sandwich was delivered a half-hour later, she ate it without stopping her work. She'd start that full life soon but not until the pain of losing Damian was no longer a sharp knife in her soul.

****

He stood at the long window of the chateau looking out into the night. Eva was an enchanting creature. Not only was she beautiful but her intelligence and humor made her the perfect companion. Having her father's permission to call on her was a bonus but even if the answer had been no, he would have continued to see her. She was a part of his soul.

The dreams erased any doubt. She came to him while he slept but as her former selves. Sometimes she was a maiden in a castle, at other times she was his young bride waiting for him to return from war. Most recently Eva had been his lover on a sparsely-populated island and he was a simple fisherman.

His parents had raised him in the faith and he knew reincarnation was only a myth. Yet he also knew they'd lived before, loved together, died and were reunited. Comfort came in knowing that after they'd left this life, their souls would meet again.

He turned at the tap of her heels heading for the salon where he waited.

"You look beautiful." He greeted her with a kiss.

"Enough that you will forgive me for keeping you waiting?"

"I'd wait a thousand years if I must."

Eva tapped his forearm with her fan and smiled. Her jewels sparkled in the gas light, shimmering nearly as brightly as her eyes. Excitement and desire stirred within him. Her father had been called away on business leaving her alone except for the servants. After tonight's soiree he would bring her home and, if she was willing, sneak back later to share her bed.

"Is she there?" Molly spoke softly as if her daughter might overhear.

"Nope, at the accountant's," Destinee answered. "So you can tell me. How are you really?"

Molly laughed. "The doctor says I'm doing quite well although I miss country fried steak and cheesecake. He assures me that before long I'll actually look forward to grilled fish and fresh fruit."

"I have a great recipe for grouper. I'll e-mail it to you. But that's not why you called."

Molly took a deep breath. "I'm worried about Jessi. She tries to stay upbeat but I think she's depressed. I know I gave her a pretty good scare but it's more than that." She paused before asking the one question she had to have answered. "Is she...are she and Damian..."

"She hasn't seen him since she got back. Or even gotten a phone call. Or one of his gifts."

Molly's heart sank and tears threatened. She'd never seen two people more in love. So what had happened?

"Did she say anything?"

"About him?"

"Yes."

"Not a word. Trust me, I've been prying."

If Destinee couldn't get her daughter to talk, she certainly couldn't. She wasn't even sure that Becky could make Jessi break.

"I don't know what to do," she admitted. "When she was little, I could kiss her booboos better but I don't have a clue how to mend a broken heart."

She hung up as discouraged as she'd been in a long time. She knew Jessi thought they'd been sneaky but Molly had been aware of when they'd come in at night. After all, she'd been young and in love once. And girls who are young and in love want nothing more than to spend every moment with their beloved.

She stared out the kitchen window, her fingers drumming against the counter top. Surely there was a solution. If only she'd asked Damian for his telephone number or even demanded his address. Looking back, she realized how evasive he'd been. When she asked where he lived, he'd said a suburb of Seattle. When she asked about his occupation, he said he was a consultant. His obvious devotion to Jessi had blinded her.

Picking up the phone again, she called her sisters and arranged for lunch. If she couldn't fix Jessi's life, she might as well see if one of them had a problem she could fix.

****

"The taxi's here!"

Jessi jumped up from her desk at Destinee's shout. She touched the locket at her neck. It had been weeks since she'd worn it yet today she needed to feel the chain against her skin. She wanted a physical reminder that once she had been loved.

Grabbing her suit jacket, she picked up a folder off the desk and tucked it into her briefcase. She rushed out with a wave of goodbye and jumped into the waiting taxi. Naturally, the line at the airport check-in was long. She moved her suitcase inch by inch until she finally reached an agent.

The flight was full. Trapped in a center seat, she gave up on trying to read and closed her eyes. Maybe

Page 265

she'd nap without dreaming.

She blinked awake as the attendant touched her shoulder and told her to prepare for landing. She was relieved that the man beside her had been sleeping, too. The grandmotherly woman at the window seat smiled and said "Welcome back" when Jessi arched her back in the only stretch she could manage in the cramped space.

Progress off the plane was slow. Jessi expected that the promised driver wouldn't be waiting at the luggage carousel considering the way her life seemed to be going. And sure enough, there was no sign with her name. She frowned, trying to remember if she had the hotel's address. Ah, she could always wait outside until she saw the right shuttle.

A voice interrupted as she reached for her black rolling suitcase.

"Let me get that for you."

A shiver of recognition prickled her skin. She turned slowly to look into unforgettable dark eyes.

"Damian?" The word came on a slow whisper.

"Yes, love." He opened his arms. Hope and disbelief mixed inside her as she fell into them, clinging to his solid body, inhaling the familiar scent of him.

Page 266

"How? Why?" she stammered, tipping her head back to study his face.

"I couldn't do it." He released her, lacing his fingers with hers as he grabbed her suitcase with his free hand.

"Couldn't do what?"

"Stay away." His voice was thick. She kept hold of his hand but held back her questions. The miracle of his presence was enough for now.

They crossed the wide blacktop to the parking structure in silence. They remained silent as they left the airport and headed into the heavy Los Angeles traffic in Damian's sleek black luxury sedan. She already knew he was an excellent driver but she still admired his skill into maneuvering the freeways. When he pulled up in front of a hotel and handed the valet his keys, she realized this was site of her meeting. In less than an hour, she would be in a room with two dozen mid-level managers discussing the perils and pitfalls of social media careerwise.

"You'll be here when I get done right?"

"Your meeting's been cancelled." He rolled her suitcase behind them as they through the door opened by the doorman.

Jessi stopped two feet inside the building.

"What do you mean, it's been cancelled? I flew halfway across the country for this."

"For a seminar hosted by Avalon Financial. It's unfortunate that I'm the only one from my company who could make it."

"Your company?"

He nodded. "I admit it. I lied. I didn't want to talk business while we were visiting your mother. And I am a consultant of a kind."

"You're the head of a company that managed to make a profit when the economy went bust. The elusive, refuses to be interviewed CEO with the golden touch."

Damian laughed. "So says the press. I'm just a working slob."

He touched her back and they began walking across the elaborate lobby to the front desk. Her mind was whirling. Okay, he was rich. And, duh, handsome. But how could have known every single blooming thing about her when they'd never met?

As reading her mind, he smiled at her and said, "I'll explain when we get upstairs."

Upstairs turned out to be a lavish suite that Jessi knew she could never afford on what she made. She'd heard the phrase "reeked of money" but hadn't really know the meaning until now. This was how he lived? And she'd taken him to the bowling alley in Michigan?

"We're here." She dropped onto the lush sofa. "Tell me. Please. I'm so confused."

And a little freaked-out if she was being honest. Her imaginary lover was real. The man she'd dreamed about for years was standing in front of her as flesh-and-bone as she was herself.

"Remember my dreams about the fair maiden?" he said.

She nodded.

"They started when I was about eight. As I grew older, they became more, uh, adult. Sometimes I visited a castle where the beautiful princess became mine or I was a fisherman. The woman in the dreams was always the same. She was always you."

"But how?"

"Because we've always belonged to each other. Last year I was at a fundraiser and there you were, the woman of my dreams in a long black dress and pearls."

"The art gallery gala. My hair…"

"…was piled on top of your head with pearl pins holding it in place. But I knew that if I walked over and pulled out those pins, your hair would be a wave of flames over your shoulder. And I also knew that if I touched you, I'd sweep you up and carry you away."

"So you stalked me?" No, he couldn't have. That was just plain creepy.

"My dreams became of you." He touched her face with gentle fingers. "Don't ask me how it's possible but while I slept, we had a courtship."

"But how did you know to come to Durkin?"

"You asked me. In my bed, in my dreams. You didn't want to go alone and face the 'poor Jessi' comments. So I went."

Jessi ran her hands through her unruly hair, trying to make sense of what she'd heard. Dream relationships were impossible. Reincarnation was impossible, yet Damian had experienced them both.

"Tell me you don't feel it and I'll leave."

She blew out a breath. The logical part of her mind told her this was impossible. The emotional part of her desperately wanted to understand.

"When did they start? The dreams about me, I mean."

"A few weeks before I went to Michigan. It's like my brain did a time jump and took me from the past to the now."

When Destinee went to the psychic fair.

"Why didn't you tell me while we were there? Why the Cinderella at midnight routine?"

Damian tensed and his face tightened. She wasn't sure she wanted to hear his answer.

"So you can live. In every dream, in every life, you carry my child and you both die. Over and over again."

Shock raced through Jessi. In her dreams, the mystery man died first leaving her alone and forlorn. And, if he was right, pregnant as well and doomed to die.

Which was absolute hogwash.

"You said yourself that this life, our life together, is happening in the present. And in the 21st century we have specialists and neonatal units. And lots of children waiting for their own family."

She stood and placed her hands on his shoulders.

"So tell me, lover, where do we go from here?"

"To lunch," he replied without hesitation. "Eventually, I hope, to the bed in the other room. And as soon as we can arrange it, back to Michigan. I have a question for your mother."

"Oh?" Jessi's heart began to pound.

"After I ask you first." He dropped to one knee and took her hand. "Jessica Flint, will you do me the honor of becoming my wife?" He smiled. "Again?"

"Oh, yes." Joy flooded through her. "Yes, yes, yes!"

Tin cans clanged in the wake of the limo carrying Damian and Jessi from the church. Nearly everyone in Durkin had shown up for her wedding or so it seemed when she'd walked up the aisle on her mother's arm. A pregnant Becky and non-pregnant Heather have been beaming in the bridesmaid dresses they'd chosen themselves. She'd barely noticed; her attention had been on Damian in his black tux. He still took her breath away, even a year after his proposal.

Her mother, in typical Molly fashion, had thrown herself into planning the perfect wedding for her only child. Although Jessi tried to rein her in, Damian became her partner in crime. She thought the dove release as they left the church was a bit much but since she'd put her foot down on Scottish pipers and being brought to her wedding in a carriage drawn by white horses.

"Now can I know the surprise?" she asked, smiling up at him.

"After the reception."

"Keep me waiting and your face won't be the only thing covered with cake before we leave."

He laughed. She traced the tiny crinkles at the corner of his eyes before tapping him on the nose.

"So now that we're married, you think you're the boss. All right then. I'll show you the brochure."

Her eyes widened at the medieval castle on the pamphlet's front.

"We're staying here on our honeymoon?"

"In keeping with our past, I've rented an entire Irish castle for the week."

"Wow." She flipped the pamphlet open and glanced inside. "Wow."

"We leave in the morning on the company jet. I

had somewhere else in mind for our wedding night."

"Here?"

"Not exactly." He flashed the wicked grin she so loved. "I've booked us the best suite in this little hotel I know. You may be the familiar with the place. It's right by a bowling alley."

She tossed her head back and laughed. Her Mr. Perfect had done it again.

The End

About The Author

Cat Shaffer, the daughter of a poet and a teacher/librarian, grew up in northwest Ohio, finally saw the light and moved to Kentucky, the land of beautiful horses and far better weather. She lives with a dignified but ultra-sneaky cat and rambunctious dog, and could not continue to live if coffee disappeared from the planet. Check out her website at www.catshaffer.com.

Did you enjoy this book?

Share your opinion by telling your friends or writing a review!

Other books by Cat Shaffer:

Keeping Secrets, contemporary romance

Bittersweet, historical romantic suspense

Kentucky Blues, contemporary romantic suspense

No Safe Place, contemporary romantic suspense

Her Hired Man, humorous contemporary romance

Dixie White and the Seven Dates,

humorous contemporary romance

www.ingramcontent.com/pod-product-compliance
Lightning Source LLC
Chambersburg PA
CBHW031706170626
46808CB00005B/1625